Her Sweetest
REVENGE
3

Also by Saundra

Her Sweetest Revenge

Her Sweetest Revenge 2

Her Sweetest Revenge 3

If It Ain't About the Money

Hustle Hard

A Hustler's Queen

Anthologies
Schemes and *Dirty Tricks* (with Kiki Swinson)

Published by Kensington Publishing Corp.

Her Sweetest
REVENGE
3

SAUNDRA

KENSINGTON PUBLISHING CORP.
www.kensingtonbooks.com

DAFINA BOOKS are published by

Kensington Publishing Corp.
119 West 40th Street
New York, NY 10018

All Kensington Titles, Imprints, and Distributed Lines are available at special quantity discounts for bulk purchases for sales promotions premiums, fund-raising, and educational or institutional use. Special book excerpts or customized printings can also be created to fit specific needs. For details, write or phone the office of the Kensington special sales manager: Kensington Publishing Corp., 119 West 40th Street, New York, NY 10018, attn: Special Sales Department, Phone: 1-800-221-2647.

Dafina and the Dafina logo Reg. U.S. Pat. & TM Off.

Published by arrangement with Delphine Publications. Previously published as *Her Sweetest Revenge 3*. First trade paperback edition: June 2014

ISBN-13: 978-1-61773-987-3
ISBN-10: 1-61773-987-1
First Kensington Trade Edition: March 2016
First Kensington Mass Market Edition: December 2018

ISBN-13: 978-1-61773-986-6 (e-book)
ISBN-10: 1-61773-986-3 (e-book)

10 9 8 7 6 5 4 3 2 1

Printed in the United States of America

This book is dedicated to the characters of
HSR3.
They have inspired me with delight to bring
them to life.
They are as close to me as family.

Acknowledgments

Father God thank you for the encouragement that makes all this possible. There would be no words without your will. Thank you to all of my family, who continue to support me book after book. To my husband and his support: we do this together. A special thanks to my editor Selena James and the whole Kensington team who help make this possible. This writing journey is awesome and always new. To all who have waited and anticipated this finale to HSR, the love I have for these characters is phenomenal. Enjoy reading it as much as I have enjoyed writing it. Strap yourself in, this ride is rocky.

Author
Saundra Jones
1 key stroke at a time

Chapter 1

We stayed in California four weeks after the shooting and everything still felt like a bad dream that I could not wake up from. For three of those four weeks, Todd was on life support, hanging on to dear life for as long as he could.

His mother, Louise, had received the bad news of him being shot over the telephone and took the first flight out to California to be by her only son's side. Upon arriving, she had been distraught past comfort, yet determined to see Todd live. After weeks of watching him lying there hooked up to dozens of machines with no change and hearing the doctor deliver the same speech to her day after day, she finally accepted the fact that there was no hope of him ever recovering. So with a calm, blank stare on her face, she reached for the pen and silver clip-board the nurse held out to her. Her hands shook violently as she signed the paperwork that sealed Todd's fate. He was gone. Rochelle was devastated. She had spent days in the hospital chapel praying. For days she didn't eat anything and she only drank liquid at the threat of the doctor hospitalizing her if she didn't. I knew without a doubt that it was my fault; no one said it, but I knew.

It was shortly after Todd died that Rochelle demanded that I tell her the entire truth about Squeeze. She had been in and out of conscious-ness when Monty had kidnapped her and she overheard Monty and me arguing. After putting two and two together, she figured out it was re-venge for what I had done to Squeeze. But want-ing to forget the entire situation she endured, she never asked, and I totally understood. But once Todd was killed, that all changed and she wanted to know everything. She said she had to make sense of why everything had happened and why every man that she loved had been killed. I told her without any reluctance, even though I understood the risk. I owed her that much. Now she knew exactly how much blood I had on my hands, including Charlene's, one of our once close friends. Who, in my opinion, had committed the ultimate betrayal—deceit. But only I looked like the monster.

Finally, after Todd's body had been shipped back to Detroit and the funeral held, life was slowly moving on. A couple of weeks had passed since the burial and I was back to work at the salon. I had to do something to keep myself busy. I just wanted to forget that I was ultimately to blame for all of the bad shit that had happened. But that was easier said than done.

"Mya." Keisha, one of Rochelle's regulars, called my name and pulled me away from my private thoughts.

I was sewing in her new round of blond-colored Brazilian hair. She wore it long down her back in big locks. She had been babbling a mile a minute and I had not heard a word.

"Damn, you daydreaming? Or your ears plugged?" she accused with sarcasm in her tone.

"Oh, my bad. I was thinking about something for a minute. What's up? What did I miss?" I chuckled to play it off. There was no way she would understand my situation.

"I was just asking when do you think Rochelle comin' in? I tried to call her the other day just to see how she was doing. She didn't answer, though."

I wanted to say, "Join the club," but I decided against it.

"Dang, what, you don't like my work or somethin'?" I joked as I stuck the needle back in to start a new row. I had to compliment myself, it was flowing just right.

"Whatever." She laughed. "Real talk, I'm just worried about my girl. That's all."

I saw the concern on her face in the mirror. Honestly, I knew how she felt. I felt the same way times ten. But I had to assure her that all was good. Rochelle wouldn't want me to say otherwise.

"I know, but she good, she just gettin' a little rest, that's all."

I reassured her with a smile. Just as I pulled the needle all the way through the track, Hood stepped in. I instantly knew something was up by the look on his face. What can I say, I know my man.

"What's up, Hood?" Keisha spoke. Her younger brother Drew worked for the Height Squad.

"What's up?" He spoke to her while looking directly at me.

He wanted to talk. It was written all over his face.

"Hey, babe, can I holla at you for a minute?" he finally said.

"Sure. Give me a second. I'll meet you in the back."

I always tried to remain professional or least I did my best. After pulling the needle completely out, I told Keisha I'd be right back.

"Ah, you straight," she said as she started scrolling through her Instagram pics.

Soon as I opened the door to the room that we use as sort of a break room, I found Hood pacing back and forth. Yeah, something was definitely up. I took a quick deep breath. Just in case I would have to ease it out slowly.

"What's wrong?" I braced myself but was still not prepared.

"It's Walt. He dead. Somebody rolled up on him at a red light on the block about an hour ago and pumped him full of bullets."

"You gotta be fuckin' kiddin' me."

I was shocked. The dude had just started running the crew and already somebody put out a hit on him. What the fuck? The game was a bitch.

"What happened? Do you know who did it?"

"Word on the streets is that it was a hit from Florida. Niggas say he was in to some people back in Florida for some big money and a murder."

"So what you gone do?" That was my new concern. I really didn't want him to get involved.

"I can't do shit about that. That was on him. His old baggage, he shoulda took care of that. He knew the rules. I hate that he even brought that shit here. He told me he was clean. But whatever, that's done."

The look on his face showed that he meant what he was saying. That was it. To be honest, I was relieved that he was not going to retaliate. Something told me that this was not it, though; he had something else to drop on me.

"Then what is it, Hood? Tell me straight out. I gotta weave to finish." I was sarcastic on purpose.

I was agitated because I knew what was coming next.

Hood put both his hands on his head and rubbed back and forth, then sighed. "Well, as you already know, Walt didn't completely have the torch yet. I had planned to turn it over to him over the next couple of weeks. So technically, it's still mine. And the streets already buzzin' non-stop."

That I was not shocked about. These streets are monstrous twenty-four seven, they stay waiting for the next move or come-up.

I folded my arms across my chest and cleared my throat. "What's your point?"

I continued to play dumb. He would have to say it. I refused to let him off the hook easy.

"I have to take the streets now before a war gears up. These niggas ready to try to claim some shit. You already know I ain't havin' it. Besides, if I don't, dead bodies gone be all over the place, innocent people included. The word new territory make these niggas buck."

As much as I hated to admit it, he was right. The Height Squad had to have their leader or Detroit would become a war zone for their spot. Niggas for the trap houses and their territory, or at least territory they would try to take over, and addicts for their next hit, because if they couldn't cop they would trip out, too. Hood had no choice. These were the hard facts. As much as I wanted to fight him on this, I could not.

"I guess you gotta do what you gotta do."

I gave in as a single tear slid down my right cheek. My husband was back in the life that he seemed not able to escape. And his fate was ultimately mine. I took my hand and wiped the tear away. There was no need for it.

"I gotta get back to Keisha."

I turned to leave, my heart in my stomach.

"Babe."

Hood reached out, pulled my left hand, and turned me toward him. He looked me deep in the eyes with nothing but love and sincerity.

"I'm sorry. But I promise you right here and right now. This is not going to be forever. I promise you that." I so wanted to believe that. But was it true?

He kissed my forehead then my lips slowly before I turned and walked away.

Chapter 2

After Hood laid that news on me yesterday, I felt mentally exhausted. I went home, climbed into bed, and slept until this morning. I wasn't depressed, just tired that so much was always coming at me. Almost like in a never-ending circle. My body had concluded that sleep would be the best method of dealing with it, and after waking up feeling fresh, I agreed. I brushed off my shoulders, pulled back my bedroom drapes, and said "good morning, world" to the sun that was shining beautifully outside. I jumped in my white Range Rover and pointed it in the direction of Rochelle's condo. It had been two full days since I had heard from her.

Pulling up to her condo, I noticed that she had her Lexus parked outside along with her new sports Mercedes-Benz truck she had copped right before our trip to California. Normally, she kept one or the other in her connected two-car garage. I jumped out of the Range and headed up to the door and pressed the doorbell. Three rings later, there was no answer so I started to knock. She knew how much I hated to wait, as I was known to be impatient. As my fist went up for round two of knocking, the door swung open.

The solemn look on Rochelle's usually happy face clearly said that she didn't want to be bothered. She pulled her baby blue Prada robe tighter around her body and asked, "Why didn't you call first?"

A slight frown rounded my face, because her question threw me off. I had never had to call before.

"Since when do I have to call first? And what took you so long to answer the door?"

I threw questions back at her since she wanted to be a grouch. Not waiting on her to give me an answer, I stepped around her into the condo. I instantly stopped. She had all the drapes drawn tightly shut. It was so dark that I could barely see in front of me to take another step. I turned to Rochelle, who then rubbed her hand through her hair.

"Look, I don't mean to be snapping on you, but I was just gettin' into a good sleep. And to be honest, I don't get that often lately," she admitted and I felt guilty.

"Sorry, I just wanted to check on you. But why all the darkness? I mean I can't see shit." I scanned the darkness again. And the results were the same pure darkness. Without answering, Rochelle hit the switch and a light came on, brightening the room. Finally, I could see and relief swept over me. Looking around the room, I saw a blanket on the couch and a cigarette tray full of ashes. It was obvious she had been sleeping and chain smoking. The smell of the smoke clouded my nostrils and filled my lungs at the same time. I coughed.

"Rochelle, what is going on?"

I was worried. I knew she had not been feeling well. But smoking packs of cigarettes back to back was not the answer. The look on her face showed her agitation just a little bit. She turned her head away from me.

"Nothing, Mya, just trying to get some sleep and relax," she stated as she pulled her robe even tighter, as if it could be any tighter. The grip she had on it was deathly and I understood why. She had the AC on frost. She headed to the sofa with the blanket, plopped down, and wrapped herself up.

"Why do you have it so damn cold in here?" I managed to say; my teeth were clicking to together from the cold.

"It helps me sleep better."

"Where is Tiny?"

I realized she was nowhere in sight. Tiny always came out of her room when Rochelle answered the door. I always joked that she was Rochelle's bodyguard.

"She's with Wynita. I'm supposed to pick her up later today. But I might let her spend one more night."

She'd had a doctor's appointment scheduled the day before. I wanted to know if he had found anything wrong with her.

"What did the doctor say?"

"Nothin' much. According to him I just need some rest. And to be honest, I agree, and that's exactly what I'm trying to do."

Throwing the blanket back, she reached for her pack of Newports off the table. She lit a cigarette, took a drag, and relief instantly displayed across her face. Pushing her hair off her face, she looked at me and exhaled. A cloud of smoke rushed the air.

"But I should be back to work soon."

"Don't worry about that right now. I want you to get better first."

I smiled at her, but she didn't smile back. Instead, she took another drag from her cigarette and released another cloud of smoke. I almost felt like those clouds were accusing me of something. But I released that crazy thought as quickly as it had come.

Suddenly I had a good idea. It had been a minute since we had been out to lunch together. Actually, it had been back before the California trip and that felt like a lifetime ago. Nothing had been normal since. Not that anything in my life ever was.

"How about we grab some lunch? I'm hungry as hell. I haven't had anything to eat since lunchtime yesterday," I admitted. After Hood had laid that information on me, I completely lost my appetite—and two pounds.

Blowing out more cigarette smoke and sitting forward on her couch, Rochelle put her cigarette out in the ashtray.

"Not today, Mya, I just want to get back to sleep. But maybe some other time."

She wrapped back up in her blanket and lay back. I almost felt like she was kicking me out and I was running out of things to say. Feeling like shit about my best friend's grief, I told her bye and bounced.

After grabbing myself a quick bite, I headed to the salon for the day. Leslie had a two-thirty appointment with me to get her hair done.

"What's up, boss lady," Pam spoke as I strolled through the door of my successful establishment.

As always, when I entered my salon I felt a bit of bliss. I was a proud business owner, because I had literally started from the bottom but now was here. I mean my life was not squeaky clean, as everybody is already aware, but I knew God was good and I had hope.

"Ain't nothin'. I'm good." I followed up. "Is everything running smoothly around here?" Since Rochelle had been off, everyone's workload had increased. But we kicked butt as a team with no complaints.

"Yeah. I just booked a squeeze-in for Fantasia Barrino. She's in town for a show and her stylist fell ill. And of course, we were referred as the hottest in town. Her bodyguard and her assistant will be bringing her by in about three hours."

"Is Trina ready?"

"Of course. She already knocked out her

first three for the morning. She just stepped out to lunch and will be back in time. And she has three more scheduled for late nights." Pam beamed.

"All right, that's what's up." I smiled as well.

The news made me happy, not only because Fantasia was coming, but because in the last six months our celebrity clientele, which included K. Michelle and Coko from SWV, to name a few, had increased through referral. My girls, Pam and Trina, were always on the top of their game. Rochelle too, when she was here. We had a good team. I was proud of that. The salon had been getting quite a buzz for being the top salon in the Detroit area. And I didn't take for granted that without my team and their efforts, this would not be possible. Hood had even suggested I think about opening up another one somewhere else. But I just wasn't sure if I was ready for that yet. My personal life needed to be a little more stable first.

"Okay, I'm going back to gear up for Leslie; she should be here soon. Just send her right back when she arrives."

No sooner than I sat my bloody-red Coach bag down and turned on my curling iron set, Leslie popped through the door.

"What's up, chic?" Leslie spoke as she glided across the floor and landed right in my chair.

"Shit, girl. Ready to lay your wig to the side." I meant every word: doing hair always helped me relax.

"I hope so because I need it. I been so busy I couldn't even get in here last week."

Yes, Leslie was one of those every-week clients. And she didn't look for a discount just because we were cool. I despised people like that. No, she paid full price on the strength for me to keep her looking fabulous.

"I know with your new dating life and all," I joked.

Leslie had recently met someone who kept a smile on her face. She kept his identity a secret, though. She had never brought him around.

"Oh no, he ain't the reason. I'm talking about the things I been dealing with, period. Things just been crazy, but it's all good, though. I'm getting it together. What about you?"

"The same old thing, coming up in here daily and gettin' it in. I been helping out with Rochelle's clients so I have been super busy. It's all good, though, because that's what we do, have each other's back."

Leslie shook her head in agreement. "I feel you. How is Rochelle doing? It's been a minute since you said anything."

"She a'ight, just gettin' lots of rest. I went by her crib today before I came in. You know Rochelle, she can't wait to get back to this salon. But I told her to chill. She don't need to be in a rush. We got her back."

"And you are right, she needs to grieve first. If she grieves properly, she will heal a lot faster," Leslie advised.

We had both dealt with the death of a loved one, so we knew what she was going through. But on the other hand, I worried about Rochelle even more because it had only been a short two years since she had lost Li'l Lo. And I personally knew that she still suffered from that, because he was truly the love of her life. Todd's death was just a thick piece of damage layered on top of that devastating pain that she was still trying to suppress.

Before I could make any more comments, my phone started to ring. The ringtone told me that it was my mom. Normally, when I'm doing hair and my phone rings, I don't answer it. But not only had she called me once, she hung up and called right back. That told me that I needed to answer. I paused for a minute to dry off my wet hands, reached for the phone, and hit the talk button.

"What's up, Ma?"

"Mya," she all but screamed through the phone. "What took you so long to answer?"

"I'm at the salon doing hair."

She should have known that. I'm always at this salon.

"Oh, I don't mean to interrupt, but I called to let you know he can come home today. They are releasing him tonight."

I almost asked who she was talking about, but when she said "they are releasing him," I knew without a doubt she was talking about Dad. My hands started to tremble. I had been waiting a long time to hear those words. Words would not come. The cat had my tongue, as they say. My heart and soul screamed with happiness.

"Mya," Ma screamed my name through the phone again. Matter of fact, she screamed so loud that Leslie heard her. I guess it took me too long to respond to the news.

"Is everything okay?" Leslie asked, making eye contact with me.

"I'm here, Ma." I spoke through choked-up tears. "Just a little shocked."

"I know, baby, me too. All of our prayers have been answered. I haven't been able to tell Monica yet, though. She is in class and has her phone off, but she'll be here in about an hour. So I will tell her then."

I knew Monica would cry. She was sensitive that way.

"Okay, ummm, what time do we need to be there to pick him up?"

"They just told me tonight. You know he has to be processed out and that can take a while. But I don't want him to have to wait around one minute after he is released. So as soon as you get done there, call me. I want you guys to pick him up. I'll wait here."

That was real talk. I understood where she was coming from.

"For real, and he won't have to wait. Soon as I'm done I'll hit you up," I agreed, then ended the call.

Leslie's eyes were glued to me. I had told her all about my dad being in prison, so I was sure she had some idea what we were talking about.

"Okay, what the hell is going on?" She held her head up and water dripped down the back of her smock.

"My dad is coming home today."

The words sounded strange rolling off my tongue. I had held my breath for six and a half years not knowing if those words would ever happen. I had prayed for this at least a million times.

"That is awesome, Mya." Leslie smiled and leaned back into the sink.

"Ohh, wait, I need to call Hood."

As if he read my mind, his ringtone chimed on my phone. Before long, I was spilling the good news on him. After a little planning, we concluded that we would head down when I was finished up at the salon. We would sit there until they released my dad through those gates. I had waited long enough. I was ready to hold my dad. If this was a dream, whoever pinched me first would get the shit slapped out of them.

Chapter 3

The ride to the prison was, by far, the longest one I had ever taken. As many times as I had visited my dad, I could not remember it taking so long. I was nervous as hell that something would go wrong and he would not be released. I barely said one word to Hood on the drive but he understood why, so he drove with his left hand and held my hand with the other. It helped to calm me down. When we finally arrived, my legs almost buckled as I climbed out of the car and they stiffly met the concrete. Eventually, I took one step in front of the other until we were inside the prison. Guards casually stood around sipping coffee and laughing at inside jokes as we quietly stood in the lobby area waiting. I wished he would hurry up and come out. I wouldn't feel satisfied until I saw his face. Nothing would be certain until that moment.

As soon as I saw his face when he strode around the corner, I knew my dreams had come true. I wanted to run to meet him halfway, but my feet were stuck to the floor.

"Baby girl," were the first words he uttered as he wrapped me tightly and securely in his arms.

I had not been held in my father's arms for a long time because these walls forbid it. I wept like a baby from the warmth and security of his embrace. The moment was surreal because I had wished for it for so long. My emotions were mixed. I was happy that I had my dad back and sad that Li'l Bo would never have this chance to see him freed from prison.

I finally found the strength to let my hands drop from around his waist and I took a step back. I took a good look at him with his tall frame. He was still strikingly handsome and he looked as though he had not aged a bit.

"Hey, Daddy." I smiled.

A single tear slid down the corner of my inner eye onto my nose, then to my top lip and into my mouth as I let out a slight laugh. I sounded like I was twelve years old. I was still a daddy's girl, and after all this time nothing about that had changed. Hood stood back and watched us reunite. He was more than aware how much this meant to my family and me. I glanced back at him and found him with a huge smile spread across his lips. He was big on family just like me; unfortunately the only family he had was his momma.

"Hood, what's up, son?" Dad glanced around with his sight set directly on Hood.

"Ain't nothin,' Mr. Lester," Hood spoke back as he stepped toward my dad.

They locked hands then patted each other on the back like guys do. I smiled; it warmed my heart to know that they accepted each other. They always shared good conversation when Hood and I went up to visit him.

"Well, are you ready to go home, Dad?" I asked for formality only. The answer was clear.

"Hell yeah, I been waitin' for years to leave this dump."

He skimmed over his shoulder for a brief second then turned back, facing me. The look on his face told me his next question before he uttered a word. Family.

"Where is your mom, Monica, and Imani?"

He viewed his surroundings as if he had just noticed that they were not there.

"They all at home. Monica was at school when we hit the highway. And Mom decided to wait at home. Come on, hop in, let's not waste another minute hanging around here." We headed to the parking lot without looking back. Hood popped the locks on his all-black Escalade as we approached. I decided to sit in the back and let Hood and Dad ride up front together. I wanted to be sure that Dad was as comfortable as he could be. Dad let the leather seats soothe him as he settled in. I could see his shoulders relax from the comfort.

"Damn, these seats feel good. It's been a long time since I sat on anything leather. And I can't lie. I miss that shit." He was stressed, but his grin never faded. Dad was used to the best of the best before he went up.

Hood looked at him and smiled. "No doubt, Mr. Lester. And rest assured, you can borrow this truck anytime you feel like you need it."

Ironically, the ride back to Detroit was quick. Before I knew it we were pulling up to the condo where Ma and Monica lived. Inside, Monica threw herself into my father's arms with so much force he stumbled backward, and that is where she stayed for at least five minutes. Her face was buried in his chest and all you could hear were her whimpers. The sight of my sister holding on to my father for dear life broke my heart, but in a good way.

A smile covered Dad's face but the tears that raced down his cheeks told me that he felt the same. Slowly, Monica released herself and started to wipe at the wetness on her face.

"I thought I would never get the chance to hug you again, Daddy," Monica admitted. "This is one of the best days of my life."

Monica rubbed at her nose and sniffed; we were both Daddy's girls.

"Mine too, sweet pea. There wasn't a day went by that my heart didn't ache to see all of you. And to be home with you all is just not real yet."

His eyes browsed the room until they found Ma, who had been standing in the same spot since we entered the condo. Realizing who he was gazing at, Monica stepped out of the way. With one immense step, Mom was in his embrace. They hugged and kissed each other as if they were the only two in the room. Monica and I looked at each other and laughed.

"Hold up, you two, there are kids in the room," I joked.

This was exactly the way I remembered them being with each other in the past, very much in love with each other and always showing affection in public. Ma was alive with him— I think that is part of the reason she suffered so much when he got locked up.

"Ummm hmmmm," Monica cosigned and we all laughed.

While laughing, Dad's eyes landed on Imani. She was standing still watching all of us. She hadn't uttered a word. Dad walked slowly over to her and lowered himself down to her level. Imani reached out and wrapped her tiny arms around his neck. Monica immediately shot a look in my direction and both of our mouths dropped open. We were in shock because Imani never went to anyone she didn't know. It was natural for her to play the shy card. But to our dismay, she warmed up to him quickly.

Dad turned to us. "Now what's that good food I smell? Who cooked?"

"Who you think?" Ma put her hands on her hip. "And I made your favorite, too, spaghetti with catfish. I even threw in sweet potatoes, so you better be hungry."

"Dang, woman, you did all that? I guess you have been waiting on me." He winked at her and rubbed his stomach. "So you just fill me up a plate because I'm starving."

"Hungry, too, Grandma," Imani said in her toddler voice.

We all started laughing.

"We all are," I followed up. "Let's eat."

While eating, we talked about some of everything from the past. There was not one person at the table who didn't have a huge grin on their face. Looking around the table, I just could not believe that we were all back together as one big family. But Li'l Bo's presence was definitely missed. To be honest, time had not healed the pain much and his name came up several times as we reminisced. The hurt was strong on Dad's face and he could not fight back the tears for much longer. So he relaxed and let them ease down his cheeks. I got up from the table to grab the Kleenex, when suddenly there was a knock on the door. We all kind of froze in our spots because not one of us was expecting company. Then Ma suddenly remembered.

"Oh, that is probably Big Nick. I called him."

Ma got up from the table, looked through the peep, then opened the door.

Big Nick stepped inside, looking only for my Dad. He handed my mom the bottle that he had cradled in his hands. Making his way around the table, Dad and Big Nick shook hands then hugged, slapping each other on the back.

"Man, it's good to have you home," Big Nick mouthed with excitement.

"It's good to be home. Man, I forgot how

fresh the air could really be. That air behind them walls is polluted."

We all laughed a little, but we knew he was serious.

Before long Dad, Hood, and Big Nick retired to the living room laughing, talking, and sipping on the Hennessy that Big Nick had brought with him. After helping Ma and Monica clean up the dishes, I decided it was time to leave. I'd had a long day and I was tired.

The sun was shining bright and I was feeling good. After eating breakfast with Hood at IHOP, I headed downtown. Monica had dropped Dad off to see his parole officer, but she had class so she needed me to swing through and scoop him up. Seeing his parole officer was my father's first order of business as a free man. He would have to abide by all types of rules and regulations, but we were all willing to do whatever we could to help. Dad was waiting outside when I pulled up.

"Hey, Dad," I spoke as he climbed inside the truck.

"What's up, Baby Girl?"

Hearing him call me that outside of those walls was strange. Normally when he called me that we were on the phone at the prison where the window blocked us from touching each other and muffled the sound. In person, it sounded clear.

"Why you standing outside?" I asked out of curiosity.

"Look, I spent enough time with law enforcement while I was locked up. While I'm free, I plan to keep my distance between them and me. So as soon as I'm done meeting with my PO, he can kiss my ass 'cause I'm outta there." He chuckled.

I laughed, too, because I didn't blame him at all.

"I feel you, Dad," I said while using my side mirror to check traffic as I eased away from the curb. Jumping back into the heavy traffic, I headed straight to the salon. I wanted to show Dad my new baby. I knew he would be proud.

Once inside, I introduced him to Pam and Trina as I showed him around the entire salon. Then we headed back to my booth area.

"I'm so proud of you, Baby Girl, this place is really nice. I mean you got it all together."

He looked around and continued to admire everything. I beamed on the inside. It felt good to know my dad approved of the salon.

"I'm also glad we are finally alone because I have been wanting to thank you for holding our family together while I was away."

"You don't have to—" I tried to speak up but he cut me off.

He held up his hand gently to silence me but it was all love.

"No, I need to say this." He paused for a brief second. "When I first got locked up, I knew things would not be good for you all at home. I knew your mom would not be able to handle things. But, like I said before, that was my fault because I pampered her. But you"—he shook his right forefinger at me—"you stepped in and stepped up to the plate. And you held this family together. Now I know we lost Li'l Bo along the way. But there was nothing you could do about that."

Tears rolled down my face as I listened to him speak.

"I am so proud to have you as a daughter. You are a force to be reckoned with, and with your strength, this family will always remain together. You have showed us the true meaning to the word family. I love you, Baby Girl."

"I love you, too, Daddy."

"Now look." I stepped away and grabbed some Kleenex off the counter behind me. "All these tears have got to stop. I am going to mess around and cry a river," I joked.

I had been crying off and on for two days. It was time to put a lid on it and enjoy this new beginning. I wanted to enjoy him being home. No more tears.

"Sorry. I didn't mean to make you cry, but that had to be said."

He turned and surveyed the room again.

"So I noticed Rochelle is not here. How is she?"

That question was bound to come up sooner or later. I was not surprised. He hit a soft spot, but Rochelle had been a part of our family forever, so I knew he cared.

"Well, she is still off. I told her to just chill for a minute."

"She still is taking it hard, huh?"

"Yeah."

I wanted to change the subject. Talking about Rochelle would only bring more tears to my eyes.

"So anyway, what's up with your parole officer? What did he say?"

He rubbed his face, letting me know that this was a stressful conversation for him as well.

"Talking about a job. 'Find gainful employment' were his exact words. Oh, and don't have no hot urine drops and keep my nose clean, of course."

"Oh, well, that sounds like normal parole officer talk to me," I said sarcastically with a smile.

"I know, right." He smiled also. "Like I need some young kid who looks like he just graduated high school supervising me."

The look on his face told me that he was not happy about that. But I decided not to dwell on that; I wanted to think positive for his sake.

"Well, I can hire you here at the salon," I offered, but my tone made it clear that it was settled.

"Hire me to do what? This place is in tip-top shape." He looked around again as if to be sure he hadn't missed anything.

"The basement is not finished at all. When Pepper, the girl that sold Hood this place, first bought it, the building was a mess. She renovated upstairs first and her plans were always to finish the basement, but she never got to it. So it's a few things down there you can do. Maybe you can turn it into a game room down there. I don't know, we'll see. I'll set you up with a budget and you get can started. I can also use you to fix a few things up here. How does that sound?"

"Sounds good to me," he agreed.

"Then welcome aboard! You can start tomorrow. I will have you fill out all the necessary new hire paperwork and you can turn it in to your parole officer. "

"Thanks for looking out. You and Hood both. Last night he gave me fifty thousand to help with a new start. I really appreciate it—without you two, things would be really hard for me out here right now."

Hood had told me the night before that he had given him the money. I had already contemplated how much money I was going to give him, but Hood had beat me to it. It was a good feeling knowing that my man was there for my family and their needs just as I was.

"We wouldn't have it any other way. All we want you to do is chill and do what you gotta do to keep your nose clean while you on parole. The one thing you must not do, Daddy, is hustle. Just stay away from it. Your family got you."

I wanted to assure him as much as I could that we had his back one hundred grand. I could only pray that he listened.

Chapter 4

As I pulled into the salon's parking lot, I noticed what looked to be Rochelle's Mercedes truck sitting outside in its usual parking space. Either that or someone was pushing a whip identical to hers and sitting in her spot. She would go ham if someone parked in her space. She could be territorial like that sometimes.

"Hey, Mya," Pam spoke as soon as I entered the doors. As usual, she was wearing a smile and looking professional. I could always count on Pam to be doing her job even when I was not around. Even though she was a noted hair stylist, she worked the hell out of the front desk when it came to customer service. That's why I paid her well. I personally wanted no one else to have that job.

"What's up?" I spoke back as I made my way

to the receptionist desk. "Is that Rochelle's car outside? Is she here?"

I looked beyond Pam as if I expected to see Rochelle standing behind her. Normally, if she had no clients and nothing else to do, she would come up front and help Pam out just so she could gossip.

Pam could see my enthusiasm. She smiled and that answered my question. "Yeah, she has like four people scheduled today."

The look on my face clearly showed that I was surprised. I had no clue that Rochelle was coming back to work today. She had managed not to inform me. And Rochelle always told me everything.

"Guessing from your facial expression, you didn't know she was here?" Pam questioned.

"No, I didn't," I reluctantly admitted.

"Well, she is back there at her booth. Lisa, her first client of the day, just left. And I gotta tell you, Rochelle is still on her A game, because girlie's hair was fierce," Pam smiled.

That made me smile as well. Even though I personally felt she needed more time off, I wanted nothing more than for Rochelle to be her old self again. But I wanted her mentally healthy first. I wished I could get her to understand that.

"Okay, I guess I'll go on back." I walked away but had to turn back for just a second. I asked, "Did those packages come in this morning? Trina needs that shampoo for her first client."

"Yes, they came in. And I shelved them before we opened."

"Thanks, Pam."

I headed straight toward Rochelle's booth area.

"What's up, chic?"

Rochelle's back was turned to me so she turned around at the sound of my voice. She was actually wearing a smile, which was more than I could say from the last time I saw her.

"Hey, I was wondering when you were going to get here."

"You know me, I'm never here early."

"This I do know." Rochelle gave another half-smile.

"So why didn't you call me last night to tell me you were coming back today?" I was feeling some type of way about that.

"I don't know. I figured Pam would let you know. Besides, I was busy getting Tiny packed up to go back with Wynita for a couple of days."

"Do you think you ready to be back?"

"Ready? Hell yes, I'm ready to be back. I was about to go crazy sitting in that damn house day in and day out drowning in my sorrows. I mean, damn, how much sleep can a bitch get?"

Now that sounded like the old Rochelle. That was confirmation that she was back to her old self.

"Rochelle, you so damn crazy."

I laughed like old times and so did she. It felt good to be us again, two best friends enjoying a good laugh.

"Pam just told me you just finished Lisa. You want to grab some lunch before your next one comes in?"

"I can't. I had Pam book me straight through.

I plan on getting out of here before dark. I don't want to overdo it. You know."

"Okay, it's cool. Well, I also wanted to let you know that Dad is out of jail. He got out a couple of days ago."

I had been so busy that I had not had a chance to tell Rochelle or take Dad by her house. Plus I didn't know if it was the best time.

Rochelle's jaw dropped in disappointment.

"Damn, Mya, why you ain't bring him by to see me?"

Her question did not shock me. Now I had to explain. "I'm sorry. I been meaning to, I just haven't had the time. He has been busy, too, taking care of a few things," I said. But really, I had not taken him by because I didn't want him to see Rochelle in the state she had been.

"So how is he then?" she asked with genuine concern.

"Good. We just tryin' to help keep his spirits up. But he seems to do that on his own. Oh, and he will be doing some work down in the basement. Part of his parole agreement is that he remains employed. So I hired him on here until he can find something else."

"That's what up, Mya. I can't wait—" Just as those few words came out of her mouth, Dad stuck his head in her area. I'm sure that Pam had told him that was where we were held up.

Rochelle was up out of her chair and hugging Dad in no time flat. In fact, she pulled a Monica on him, hugging him so tight that he stumbled. I was not shocked, though. Rochelle had been in our lives since she was young. When her father died, my dad became like a second father to Rochelle. He loved her and she loved him. After Rochelle finally released Dad, she wiped at her face, which was wet with tears.

"I can't believe that you are back. You know, Mya just told me all of a few minutes ago." Rochelle threw me under the bus.

"Dad, I told her we all been busy," I said in my defense.

"She always got an excuse." Rochelle smiled, but the smile felt like it was blaming me.

"Don't worry about it. It's all good. I was going to have her bring me out to see you as soon as I had a free minute. You know how it is when you get out of that place. You feel like you have a thousand errands to run and you want to run them all right then." Dad chuckled. "When I am going to get a chance to meet little miss Tiny?"

Rochelle had Tiny after Dad went to prison so he had never met her. A lot had changed while he was inside. We had all grown up in so many different ways. Before he went to prison, we were all spoiled little girls running around with not one care in the world, except maybe what outfit we were wearing to school next.

Just as I was about to speak again, Pam came in to notify Rochelle that her next appointment had arrived. We would have to finish up this little reunion later.

"All right, Rochelle, I will chat with you later. I'm going to show Dad the basement."

"Cool," she answered before spinning in Dad's direction. "I guess I will be seeing you later around the shop, Mr. Lester."

"No doubt," Dad approved.

I grabbed his hand and led him to show him his new work assignment area. This type of job would be different from what he was used to. No fast money involved, but it was safer. And not one day in jail was attached to it.

"Babe, do you want your eggs scrambled or over easy?" I asked Hood as I threw butter in the hot skillet.

I had woken up with the taste for some home-cooked breakfast. And a home-cooked breakfast sounded like a good idea since neither Hood nor I had to run right out the door first thing. The grits were cooling on the stove and the T-bone steaks had just come off the griddle. The only thing left were the eggs, and for the most part we both like them scrambled. However, sometimes Hood wanted his over easy, so I was giving him his choice.

"Go ahead and scramble them. It seems to go better with the steak."

Hood sat down and poured himself a cup of orange juice from the carton of Tropicana that he had just retrieved from the fridge.

I happened to agree with him, scrambled eggs rocked with a juicy T-bone. After giving the scrambled eggs one last beat in the bowl, I threw them into the hot skillet. The sizzling sound made my stomach growl. I was ready to dig in.

"So, Dad started doing some measuring down in the basement yesterday. We haven't decided exactly what he will do down there, but I guess the first thing to do is to finish it."

"Yeah, I agree. I think he could make it look pretty fucking wicked, depending on the theme, maybe some fresh paint with some designs. Don't try to boss him, though, babe. Let this be his project."

Pulling the skillet away from the hot burner on the stove, I lightly poured the eggs onto a waiting plate. Turning to Hood, I twisted up my mouth. "Are you trying to say that I'm controlling?"

"Awww, come on, babe." Hood grinned. "You know I don't think you bossy." He playfully lied his way out of it.

"Yeah, right. I love the way you sly your way out of things." I smiled back at him.

Hood always told me that I was headstrong, which was his way of saying that I was bossy. But he always let me get my way in the end.

"But real talk, I think this will be good for him," Hood said as he picked up his knife and fork.

He eyed his plate with a hunger stare as I sat it down in front of him. I could see the steam rising off his plate going straight up his nose. Without another word, his knife went straight into his steak. I could not wait to fix my plate. It was going all the way down.

"I just hope it all works out. This could be good in more ways than one."

I grabbed my plate and headed to the table.

"Babe, bring the Heinz 57 sauce," Hood asked as he forked some eggs into his mouth. The motion of his jaws told me he was savoring every taste.

Sliding into my chair with my plate full, I dug in. I was halfway through with my breakfast when the doorbell rang. I looked at my cell phone, which was sitting right next to me. Leslie was supposed to be stopping by because she had something that she wanted to talk to me about. According to the time, she was about thirty minutes early.

I looked at Hood as he shoved the last piece of hash brown into this mouth.

"Can you get that? It should be Leslie, she was supposed to be stopping by."

"No, actually that's Lonzo. He supposed to be dropping me off some papers about ten-thirty." Hood checked his watch for confirmation.

"Oh," I replied.

Hood wiped his mouth with a paper towel and stood up just as the bell rang again.

"Hold up, impatient-ass nigga," Hood yelled as he made his way out of the kitchen.

Lonzo was one of Hood's peons. Since Hood had fully taken the Height Squad back over, he had become like Hood's right-hand man. From what I could remember, Lonzo was an okay dude. I would say he was always laid back, but had strong opinions. He was also very attractive, dark chocolate with a bald head and white teeth. He was about six foot three and weighed about two hundred forty pounds and it was all muscle. Young dude, about twenty-six, I think. He was always cool with Hood, so much so that in the past when Hood considered stepping away from the Height Squad, I would have thought that Lonzo would have been a prospect for Hood to pass the crew down to. But, for whatever reason, he didn't. Hood liked him, though, so I know it wasn't personal. I guess Hood didn't think he was ready. But lately he had been giving him a lot of responsibility.

As I stood up from the table, Hood and Lonzo rounded the corner.

"What's up, Mya?" he spoke first. Like all Hood's workers, he was always respectful.

"Hey, Lonzo."

I did not like them coming to my house, but Hood kept it at a minimum, so I tolerated it.

"Man, y'all got it smelling good up here. Make a brother hungry." He rubbed his stomach.

"Blame your boy Hood. Had he told me you were coming, I would have threw you a steak on the grill."

"That nigga straight." Hood chuckled. "We got some cold-ass orange juice right there if you thirsty," Hood joked, pointing at the Tropicana carton.

"Nah, I'm straight." Lonzo laughed.

I started to clear away the table as they started talking. It was time to get down to business.

"Did you bring it?"

"Yeah, I got them right here."

Lonzo pulled some papers out of his back

pocket and put them into Hood's anxiously waiting hands. Hood looked them over and started shaking his head in agreement.

"That is what you needed, right?" Lonzo asked. "You straight, right?" he pushed.

Hood still didn't answer right away; his attention seemed to be on the papers that he had in his hand.

"Dawg, they straight?" Lonzo asked for the third time. His persistence was becoming annoying.

Hood finally looked up from the papers. "Fo sho, man, they what I needed. Now I want you to take the car down to Lansing first thing in the morning. Take Trey with you, he good to have if you get in a tight spot. No screwups. Got it?"

"No worries, I got you."

Lonzo held up his head and slid both his hands into his pockets.

"But what about the new bitch—Quad? You know she running that new crew called Brief Squad. Some of them li'l niggas be buck."

"Man, look, I ain't worried about that as long as they stick to the code. They already got blocks to trap. First one gets out of line, dead 'em on sight. So it is in her best interest to keep her crew in line. Female or no female, she better know her position 'cause I ain't taking no shit. Anybody subject to get bodied, even that bitch. That shit clear?"

Hood's words were monstrous but his tone was calm as he folded the papers in his hands. I was kind of shocked at Hood calling that female a bitch. I had never heard him use that term when it came to a female. But I guess when it came to the game, respect went straight out the window. I wondered about this female, though. I had never heard about a female heading up a crew. The doorbell broke my thoughts. Lonzo had decided to take Hood up on his offer and grabbed a glass for orange juice. Leaving the dishwasher open, I headed to the door.

"Hey, girl."

Leslie had a huge grin on her face as soon as the door swung open.

"Damn, I guess you in a super good mood." I returned her smile as I stepped to the side so that she could enter.

"What is that smell. Did you cook?"

"Yep, sure did."

I closed the door behind her as she stepped inside.

"I wish you had told me. I would have shown up in time to eat."

"I'm sure you would have. That is why I didn't tell you," I joked. "Come on into the kitchen. I was just about to finish loading the dishwasher.

When we walked into the kitchen, Hood and Lonzo stopped abruptly like they didn't want us to hear what they were talking about. I knew that they would not talk in front of Leslie. No outsiders. I was only getting an earful because being Hood's wife meant that I could be trusted. To not trust me could be a problem.

"Hi, Hood," Leslie spoke.

"Aye, what's up, Leslie? How you been?"

"Cool, just going to school and taking care of Li'l Rob."

"That's what's up," Hood commented.

"Hood, don't you think you should introduce them? Don't be rude, babe."

"Oh, my bad. Leslie, this Lonzo. Lonzo, that is Leslie."

Lonzo knew Rob, but he had been a small peon in the squad around the time he was murdered.

"Hey." Leslie eyed Lonzo quickly.

"Yo, what's up, ma," Lonzo spoke with swag.

I smiled at both of them. They seemed like two schoolkids meeting each other for the first time.

"It was nice seeing you, Leslie," Hood said before telling Lonzo to follow him into the den.

"It was nice seeing you, too," Leslie threw back as she walked over to the table and sat down.

"Anyway, what was so important that you had to drive all the way out here? Because you always complaining about coming out here in the 'sticks,' as you call it." I teased her.

I loved living so far out. The neighborhood was amazing. The fewer corner stores, the better.

"Girl, don't do me. You know it is true that you live in the damn country." Leslie laughed while pushing her hair out of her face.

"It is far as hell," I admitted with a grin. "But what's up?"

"Well, as you know, I have been seeing this new guy for a while." She was all smiles.

"Yes, the guy that I don't even know his name

yet. But that is another story for another day, so go ahead."

I was sarcastic on purpose. I continued listening as I loaded the dishwasher.

Leslie looked at me and playfully rolled her eyes.

"Anyway." She popped her mouth. "We have been getting closer, and as you already know, I have been talking about having a new start for a minute. And so I was thinking that this could be it. Maybe Li'l Rob and I can move to Chicago with him."

"Wait a minute, let me get this straight. You're saying you are gonna move in with this guy in Chicago? And you will be living . . . in Chicago?"

I know I said the word "Chicago" twice, but I just wanted to be sure. Because this sounded crazy to me. As far as I knew, she had not known the guy that long.

"Yes, I would move to Chicago and live with him," she clarified, like it was no big deal. "We are going to get a place together."

"Hmmm. Okay, well, if you are asking my opinion, I would say it is way too soon for that. You haven't even been dating this guy for a year. Hell, you ain't been knowing him for a whole year. Unless you ain't telling me something."

I was being straightforward. No bullshit needed.

"Not quite. But, Mya, he is a good guy and he is already set up financially."

When she said "set up" my eyes grew big. She knew what I was thinking, so she cleared it up.

"Wait, not that type of set up, he has a job. He's educated with a college degree and all."

I swallowed on that one because I knew how she was about Rob when he was down. Rob being in the dope game was the big reason why they kept breaking up.

"All that sounds good, but the fact still remains that you don't know him that well. I really think you should consider this a little longer before making a decision. This is a huge step. Not only will you be leaving Detroit, your hometown. You will be moving to Chicago, where you basically know no one. I'm just saying." I shrugged my shoulders as Leslie watched me.

I cared about Leslie, so I had to keep it one hundred with her. And I just didn't think it was smart to pack up and move to another state with a guy she hardly knew.

"Just give it a little more thought is all I'm saying."

"I'll think about it. And thanks for being real and not saying what I wanted to hear."

"No problem. We are cool and I would want you to at least hear me out."

I wanted to be clear about that. Losing Rob had been enough trauma in her life. So I had spoken my piece; I could only hope that she listened and made the best decision for herself and her son. A lot of times, people let the heart and emotions make those important decisions.

Chapter 5

"Hey, sis." Monica reached out and hugged my neck. She had some downtime from school this morning so we agreed to meet up in the mall and do a little candle and accessories shopping before I headed in to the salon. I loved to spend any time I could with my sister. We always seemed to be busy and never able to coordinate our schedules. Needless to say, all of the time we spent together was priceless.

Returning her snug hug, I took a step back and looked at her. I was always shocked at how she was growing into such a sophisticated young woman. She was no longer my baby sister and I hated to admit it, but that didn't stop me from treating her that way. No matter how hard I tried, I just could not seem to let her be an adult. I was working on it, though. Ma had even told me to ease up a little. "Ain't you lookin' all cute this morning?" I complimented her outfit.

She rocked a navy strapless wide-leg jumpsuit with a pair of G by Guess Luzter T-strap thong sandals. She looked too cute. I smiled at her as she playfully modeled for me.

"Oh, this old thing?" She played modest with a grin. "I just threw it on because it's easy and comfortable. But I also knew I would look good in it."

"Shut up." I playfully nudged her shoulder.

"So where you want to start first? Yankee Candle or Macy's?" Monica asked.

She swung her loose ponytail off her shoulder with her right hand while balancing her Calvin Klein monogram tote bag on her left wrist. I swear she could hit the runway because she had the strut down. I hadn't seen one celebrity who could balance a bag on a wrist like her.

I decided after looking around at all the foot traffic that it didn't matter where we went first. I hated finding my way through a bunch of impatient people. Mall shoppers were always impatient and their attitudes could suck if they felt you were trying to get in front of them or something. But I could give the "try it" look that made any shopper second-guess stepping to me. I didn't live in the Brewster anymore, but I could have a flashback in a minute and pop off.

"You decide wherever you want to start. Shit, I thought this time of day the traffic wouldn't be as heavy." I breathed a sigh of agitation. "Especially since everyone keep screaming about how bad the economy is."

"Hmmph." Monica laughed out loud. "Maybe they are all liars. Either way, I'm ready to shop. Let's head into Macy's first. I can't wait to sample the sunglasses."

The atmosphere inside Macy's was cool and calm. The MAC makeup ladies in the cosmetic section were standing around making up each other's faces. The ladies in the perfume area were stocking the glass cases like they physically mixed the chemicals themselves. Every employee in there looked like a mannequin. The atmosphere was just the way I liked to shop. If only they offered wine, I would be in heaven. Before heading over to the sunglasses we stopped and sniffed the perfumes. It wasn't like shopping in the hood, where you get hounded as if you gone steal the bottle as you test the perfume. No, they welcomed you to it. I loved it.

When we finally reached the sunglasses, Monica thrived.

"I swear, Mya, I love them all."

Her eyes gleamed so much from admiration that I could see myself in them. The girl truly loved to shop.

"I'm sure you do."

I had spoiled Monica the same way my father had spoiled us before he went to prison. I remembered him buying whatever we asked for and more. Christmas was crazy stupid. I'm talking about gifts touching the ceiling in our apartment. Man, I missed those days. The saleslady pulled out shades at our request and we tried them on. They were so comfortable, I felt like I could sleep in them.

Monica was looking in a mirror admiring herself in a pair of Michael Kors Blue Grad. I could tell that she was feeling them.

"So I have been thinking." She repositioned the sunglasses on her face and posed.

She didn't say anything for a minute, so I edged her on as I tried on some Ray-Bans.

"Are you going to tell me what you have been thinking about today or tomorrow?" I was sarcastic on purpose.

"Oh, my bad. Like I was saying, I have been thinking about maybe moving out and finding me and Imani our own spot."

"Really?"

"Yeah, I think it's time. Now that Dad's home, he and Mom could use some alone time to re-connect. Not that I feel like Imani and I are in the way, I know they love having us there, especially Dad, since he can see Imani every day and bond with her. But what if they want to run around the house naked?"

That statement made me discontinue examining myself in the mirror.

"That was information overload, Monica. I did not need that image in my head, now or ever."

"Sorry," she apologized, and we both laughed.

All in all, I agreed with her. Mom and Dad could use some time alone. After all, they had years of absence to make up with each other. But I also knew that Mom and Dad would not want Monica and Imani to leave just yet.

"I agree with you, that it is not a bad idea."

Monica looked at me as if she was shocked.

She was probably expecting me to go ham, blow up, and tell her she shouldn't move.

"Wait a minute, you mean you ain't gone trip or snap out?" She popped her fingers.

"Hold up, what you trying to say?" I played at being offended. "Do not act like I'm always trippin'."

"Ahh, you do, crazy lady." Monica rolled her eyes and popped her mouth.

"You and that damn Hood, always accusing me of being controlling."

"That is because you are. I totally one hundred percent agree with my brother-in-law."

"Okay, okay, I see. Well, you betta call your brother-in-law up here to pay for them sunglasses then." I pretended like I was walking away.

"All right, all right." Monica grabbed me and pulled me back to the sunglasses. "You are so not crazy or controlling. Just the best sister a girl could ever hope for."

"Yeah, yeah, I'm sure. Now I'm the best." I laughed.

I loved these playful moments with her. It always made me remember the times she, Li'l Bo, and I played together. We would have so much fun.

"But I agree with you." I got back on track with our original discussion. "Only I think you should wait until school gets out for the semester. Because you might have to make some changes with Imani's childcare depending on the area you move to."

"Right." Monica shook her head to agree

with me. "I thought about all that. So I'll start looking around and kind of gettin' some ideas to see what will fit."

"Good idea. But you not moving nowhere near the damn ghetto, so don't even think about it."

I was serious. The last thing I wanted was her and Imani dodging late-night stray bullets.

"Look, I have to get what my money can afford, but no, I don't plan to move to the ghetto. I'm going to be getting a part-time job with AT&T. I already talked with someone I know who is hooking me up."

She was excited just talking about it.

"Now, that I don't agree to."

Here I was being controlling again, but I had to speak up.

"Monica, like I have said a thousand times, you need to focus on school. Working will only complicate things, another responsibility. Don't worry about bills. I will pay them; you don't have to sweat that," I assured her.

"Here you go." Monica threw her hand in the air and shook her head side to side. "I thought you said you were not controlling. Mya, I appreciate it, but I have to be responsible for Imani and me. You do everything for us. I can do this and I promise I won't allow it to affect my schoolwork. I'm going to finish school, I promise."

At this moment, my head was as hard as a rock. I refused to allow her to work.

"Look, my mind is made up and I say NO.

Trust me, Monica, it's for your own good. Can't you see that you are going to have something that no one else in our family has? A college degree. That's priceless."

I had tears forming in my eyes.

Monica caved. "All right. But as soon as I finish school, I am getting a job."

"I should hope so 'cause I ain't gone take care of your grown ass," I joked and we both laughed.

"Enough about that and on to another subject. When we gone hit the club? All this schoolwork and no play is gettin' boring. Hell, I do like to have fun."

I was forever forgetting that she was an adult. But she never had a problem reminding me.

"Oh, so you are ready to party with the big dawgs, huh? All right, I got you. I will let you know soon and you better be ready."

"Don't worry, I'm ready to let loose. All those books have turned me into a genius. If I don't have any fun soon, I'll crack." She held out her tongue and let her eyes roll around in the back of her head to be funny.

"Stop." I laughed. "Before you end up stuck like that. But not to worry, baby sis, I got you."

We tried on shades for another hour before we finally made up our minds. By the time we were done, I had dropped a grand on shades for Monica and me like it was candy. Monica walked away with those Michael Kors Caicos 57 in Blue Grad. They were cute and, according to her, they matched her outfit, so she slid them on.

She also got a pair of BVLGARI shades. I also grabbed a pair of those—they were hot. Right before I handed the saleslady my Black card, my eyes found a pair of Burberry Grey Grad Pol that I put on before leaving the store as well.

Happy with our choices, we skipped over to Yankee Candle, where I dropped another five hundred on candles. As usual, we picked up Mom a few scents. Citrus Tango and Exotic Bloom were some new spring scents and I grabbed one of each, along with some summer scents. Yep, she too would be happy.

The salon's lobby area was unusually crowded. There were three females who were regulars standing at the reception desk, their faces showing signs of confusion and agitation. There were several phone lines ringing and Pam, who normally had it all together, looked frazzled, but she was still wearing a smile. Something was up.

"Stylz by Design, hold please." She repeated that line for the next four calls.

I wasted no time in stepping behind the counter. I whispered to Pam, "What's going on?"

"Everything," was her quick response.

She eyed the three women standing at her desk. I knew she wanted to speak to me in private, but the last thing we wanted to be was rude to customers, especially regulars.

"Let's step in the back for a minute," I whispered.

Turning to face the clients I asked, "Ladies,

can you give us just a minute? We will be right back."

As soon as were out of sight of the women, Pam, who was leading the way, turned to face me. She got so close that I could smell the Reese's peanut butter cups that she had been eating.

"Rochelle is gone. She had all of them scheduled for appointments and she just up and left, out of the damn blue."

Now it was my turn to look confused.

"What do you mean she left?"

"I mean she gone," Pam repeated without question. "She came in here this morning and did her first client of the day, that Tiffany chick. Next thing I know, she comin' out of the back with her purse and keys. She didn't even stop at my desk. She just said out loud in passing that she was leaving. She was walking so damn fast wind hit me in the face as she passed by. I yelled to ask her are if she was coming back, and without even looking back at me she said she didn't know."

I couldn't believe what Pam was saying; this didn't sound like Rochelle. I tried to grasp it all, but apparently Pam was not finished.

"Five minutes after she leaves, her next appointment shows, or least that's who I scheduled for an appointment. Because the next people that came through the door said they had scheduled appointments with her at the same time. I knew that couldn't be right because I didn't schedule them. According to them, Rochelle booked their appointments."

I threw my hand up. I needed to make sure I understood what she was saying. Why would Rochelle schedule these appointments, then skip out on them? This was part of the reason I wanted her to take some more time off. The only logical reason was that she was not ready to work again.

"Are you telling me that all of them think they have appointments right now?"

I asked this question even though I knew the answer. For some reason I wanted to make an excuse for Rochelle walking out, but I knew better.

"Yes." Pam folded her arms.

"Shit," I finally said.

I was big on customers getting the best service, so this was not okay. I took in a deep breath. The last thing I wanted to be was angry, especially with Rochelle, because I knew she was going through something. I just wished she had listened to me and hadn't tried to make herself come back so early. But I could not dwell on that; the problem was here and I needed to fix it.

"Okay, I'll take care of this. What about Trina? Is she here?"

"Yes, she has a client in right now."

I should have known that, but I wanted to exhaust all options.

"What time is Trina's next appointment?"

"In two and a half hours."

This is why I needed Pam: she carried all the information with her, not just when she was sitting in front of the computer.

"I got it, and this is what we will do. I will

take one now; once she is under the dryer, I will grab the next one. Then I will have Trina fit the other one in while her appointment is under the dryer. You get back to the calls on hold and I will come out and get the first girl."

"Sounds good to me. Let's work." Pam was amped just like me. She wanted the issue resolved. The customers must come first.

"Have them take a seat while I go tell Trina the plan. I will be up in a minute."

"Cool," Pam said, then stepped past me, heading toward the front. "Oh yeah, your dad came in, but he left. He told me to tell you that he stepped out with Big Nick."

"All right," I answered without a second thought. I had other fish to fry at this moment.

After laying the plans on Trina, I grabbed the first client and went to work. Before long, five hours had passed and all three clients had left the salon happy and satisfied. Rochelle was on my mind the entire time that I was doing heads. I still could not believe that she had walked out like that. She had not called me and said a thing as to why she did it. Rochelle always told me everything. But things were slowly changing in our friendship and I did not like it all. Since she would not call me, I picked up my cell and hit Rochelle, but the phone just rung until it went to voicemail but I was not surprised. I could barely remember the last time she had answered one of my calls.

When I got home, Hood was already there, sitting in the den. It was another surprise, but definitely more welcome than the one I got earlier. I wished it could be like this every day but I would not torture myself with this hope. It only pissed me off and started arguments that I did not want in my marriage.

"Babe, why you home so early?" I asked as I bounced down on the sofa next to him.

"No reason, I just came to the crib. Another one of my spots got hit tonight."

"For real. Why you ain't out there seeing what's up?"

"Shit, I'ma let Lonzo handle that shit. He knows what to do. He got to learn how to handle these small situations, so I gave him a li'l string."

Hood was calm. He didn't seem upset at all. If you ask me, since he had been back in the game he didn't seem interested. I mean he still ran things with a fine-tooth comb, but something was missing.

"How was your day?" he asked.

"Crazy. Just like yours."

I sat up and started to take off my shoes. My feet were killing me. I had been wearing six-inch heels all day, mainly because I had not planned to be doing heads.

"Well, I met Monica just like I planned this morning. That went good. Then I get to the salon and shit is bananas. Rochelle done up and left out of the blue, while she had clients scheduled. But, babe, the crazy part is she set all of the appointments up at the same time. So they all showed up ready to get their hair fixed. It was crazy."

"Damn, she walked out like that." I could tell Hood was also surprised. "That don't sound like your girl."

"Hmmph," I sighed. "I know, and I don't know what to think about it. I tried calling her and she didn't answer the phone. I just don't know." I shrugged.

"Babe, you just got to give her time."

"I know, Hood, but she won't talk to me. I tried to call her and she don't answer my calls and she never tries to call me."

"She needs time, Mya. But instead of calling her all the time, maybe you need to go to her."

"I know and I will. I just feel helpless."

"Everything gone be cool, stop worrying about it. What you gone do about the salon, though?"

That was a good question. I had been thinking about it on the drive home. I contemplated what I should have done a while ago. I just hadn't been ready to take that step. Sometimes, those type of decisions are hard.

"I'm thinking about gettin' another stylist in there. Honestly, I should have already done that. I have the extra space but I just don't want a ghetto salon with a thousand females in there doing hair. But I have to get someone. I have no choice, Rochelle and I can't continue to run it on our own. Our customers deserve the best service."

Hood shook his head in agreement. "Well, this might be your best option right now. You can't allow the business to sink while you on the rise. Business is at its best right now so you gotta do what you gotta do. You a boss, baby, you can do it. At least until Rochelle come back."

"No, I need one permanent person. Business is booming and I don't want the girls to become overwhelmed. So whoever I chose, I'm going to keep. Whenever Rochelle comes back, I'm sure she will be able to adapt."

At least I hoped she would, but I would worry about that when the time came.

"You do what you got to," Hood agreed.

My mind was made up. I would hold interviews so I could find the next best stylist that Detroit had to offer. I did not know how the other girls would take the news—it had been just us since I had opened the doors a few years back. But things changed and I hoped they understood that.

Chapter 6

It had been two days and I had not heard one word from Rochelle. All of my calls went unanswered. I had enough; it was time for me to do a pop-up. Inside my head, I was hearing Hood's voice say to give her time, but I was getting pissed. How much time could one person need? Hell, I was not some stranger. Today was the day.

I banged on her door but she didn't answer. I thought about using my spare key but I had left it home. I never put it on my keychain when she gave it to me. My next thought was to kick the door open. Just when I was about to do it, the door slowly opened. I didn't see anything until I looked down and saw that Tiny had opened the door. Thank God it was me and not some psycho killer.

Not wanting to show the worry on my face, I smiled as I stepped inside the condo.

"Hey, sweetheart, where is your mom?" I said as I closed the door behind me.

"She in her room asleep." Tiny smiled.

I smiled back at her as I let my eyes roam in disappointment. Toys and clothes were everywhere. I slowly looked around. This was not how I was used to seeing Rochelle's house. It was always clean, but that was not all. I got a glimpse of the kitchen and saw that cereal boxes were open on the table and bowls were on the counter; it was a mess. Without a doubt, I could tell that Tiny had been feeding herself. With my eyes still fixed on the kitchen I asked, "Tiny, are you okay?"

"Yes," Tiny answered.

Her sweet voice made me turn to face her. That is when I got a good look at her head. Her hair was a mess. Rochelle always kept Tiny's hair nothing less than perfect. Her hair always looked just like the girls on the Just For Me relaxer box at all times. Rochelle took pride in it.

"You want to play with my dollies?" Tiny got my attention.

I forced a smile. "Not right now. I need to speak with your mom, okay? Sit down and watch television until I'm through."

I slowly made my way around the corner off the living room area and down the hallway. The mess in the living room continued down the hall. I almost trampled over Tiny's Baby Alive doll. It was clear she had been having a ball with her toys.

I decided against knocking when I reached Rochelle's room. I figured just going in was my best option. She hadn't been answering my calls; what if she decided not to let me in her room. I was not going to take the chance. Slowly opening the door, I saw the light from the television and I heard the sound, even though she had it very low. I looked to the left and found Rochelle in the bed. From where I stood, I could see that she was not asleep. She was wide awake, her attention on the television, but I knew that she was not really watching it.

Without saying anything, I went all the way inside the room and stood by the edge of her bed. Seeing her like this broke my heart. Tenderly I asked her, "Are you okay, Rochelle?"

Surprisingly, she looked at me briefly, then turned her attention back to the television. For a second I thought she would not answer me.

"I'm fine," she said with no real emotion.

"I have been calling you for days."

"Well, I guess it's about time you took time out of your busy life to come see about me."

Rochelle's tone was accusing and sarcastic. That shocked me just a little bit, but I decided not to take it personally.

"I have been at the salon taking care of your clients and mine. Today was actually the first day that I had some free time, so I came right over."

I didn't know why I was explaining myself, since she was the one who had run off from the job and called no one. I thought she should have been thanking me for picking up where she left off.

"I didn't ask you to do that. You act like them bitches gone die if they don't get their hair done!" Rochelle yelled, then threw the remote across the room. That caught me by surprise.

"What's up, Rochelle? Why you trippin'?"

Rochelle swiftly climbed out of the bed, stood up, and snatched the cover off. She started to make up the bed erratically.

"Ain't nothin' wrong with me," she answered, never giving me any eye contact.

She continued to spread the comforter about the bed; she was not satisfied with the way it looked so she started it over.

But I was not accepting her answer. I was tired of being nice, because she was going out of her way to be rude.

"Bullshit, Rochelle, you over here throwing tantrums and shit!"

"Whatever." she sighed and grinded her teeth. "What is it that you want? Why are you here?"

"Why do you think? I came by to check on you and Tiny."

"Well, you came, you checked, and you saw. Now you can get out. Hell, I need to be alone." Rochelle continued to give me attitude.

"How you gone be alone, or did you forget that Tiny was even here? By the way it looks in that fucking living room and kitchen, Tiny has been taking care of herself," I accused, not caring what Rochelle thought. It was time she heard some truth.

That got her attention. She stopped making

up the bed and faced me. I had pushed a button, probably the wrong one.

"Mind your own business, Mya. And stop worrying about Tiny, she my daughter and I will take care of her. Trust me, we good over here. Now for the last time, GET OUT!" she screamed. Everything in her tone said that she meant it.

I could not believe this was happening. Rochelle had never treated me like this before. I looked at the door to her room then back at her, but I made no effort to exit. This angered her more.

"Oh, I see. You worried about me coming back to the salon to do hair for them spoiled bitches. Don't you worry, I will be back. Just tell them to give me a few minutes, if they don't mind."

I could not believe that she was serious right now. There was no way she was close to being ready to come back to work. I was sure of that.

"Are you crazy? Ain't no way you ready to come back to work! You stay home for a while. You need some time off. I told you this before and you didn't listen. But this time I insist. It's approved."

I turned to leave, but before I reached the door, I turned around and looked straight at her. I wanted her to know that I was very serious about what I was about to say.

"And don't worry, I'm leaving—but I'm taking Tiny with me."

I had seen enough to know that Rochelle was not in any condition to be taking care of her right now.

Rochelle jumped across the bed and stood in the doorway.

"Are you fuckin' stupid right now? You ain't takin' my baby nowhere, Mya. Don't do me."

I got in her face. I wanted to be sure she heard me and understood.

"I am taking her to Ms. Wynita and you can sit here and pout, bitch, and moan alone. And when you get it together, you know where she will be. Now get out of my way."

I pushed past her, bumping her shoulder a bit. She stumbled backward just a bit, then caught her balance and yelled at me as I walked out of her room.

"Kiss my ass and get out my house."

I went into Tiny's bedroom and grabbed her a few outfits, underclothes, and shoes. I found Tiny in the living room still playing with her dolls. She looked up at me when she noticed me in the doorway.

"Hey, Auntie." She smiled at me. "Are you done talking with Mommy?"

I walked toward her. "Yes, and she wants you to go with Auntie. I'm going to take you to Granny Wynita."

"Yay!" She jumped up and down and her eyes lit up. She loved her granny and Ms. Wynita loved her. I knew she would be happy that I brought her.

"I can't wait. What about Mommy, is she going?"

"Mommy is coming later, okay? She has to get some rest."

"Okay. Can I take my dollies?"

"Yep, so go ahead and grab them."

She took no time collecting them and stuffing them in a Hello Kitty tote bag. When she was done, she took her free hand and reached for my outstretched hand, and we headed out the door. As I started to close the front door, I heard Rochelle slam her bedroom door shut. She didn't even come out to tell Tiny good-bye.

Chapter 7

After two days of hair auditions, I finally picked the new stylist that would be working at the salon. Her name was Nora Hastings. I know her name sounded wack, but the bitch had crazy hair game. Over sixty stylists from all over Detroit had come to the auditions, and to be honest, they were all pretty good. But Nora was bad. She specialized in everything: cuts, sew-ins, braids, makeup. You name it, she did it. I made my decision without thinking twice. She was what the salon needed.

I saw Leslie exiting her car as I was pulling into Red Lobster's parking lot. We had decided to meet for lunch and a quick chat. We had been hanging out a lot lately, but no one took the place of Rochelle.

"See, you was saying I was gone be late."

I shut my door and hit the alarm on Hood's Bentley. I had decided to jump in it for the day. The car needed some attention because Hood never gave it any. I couldn't remember the last time he took it out for a spin.

"I guess you getting better with time," Leslie joked.

According to her, I'm always late. Even though I never agreed with her, she was right, I was known for being late. But I was on time today, so I decided to take full credit.

"Dang, I see you ridin' Bentley today." Leslie admired the car.

"Yep, I thought I would pull it out today."

I pulled on the doorknob and made my way inside Red Lobster, Leslie following. The dark lighting inside forced me to pull off the BVLGARI sunglasses that I was rocking.

"Girl, ain't nothin' wrong with that."

The hostess asked us where we wanted to be seated. The answer to that was easy for both of us: a booth inside the bar area, since it was cocktail time. As soon as a waitress approached our table, I ordered of my favorite cocktail, a Triple Berry Sangria. I could not wait to take my first sip. I almost craved it.

"So I have officially chosen the new stylist. Her name is Nora and she has crazy hair game." I was excited about my choice.

"Wait, did you say her name is Nora?"

"Yes, Nora Hastings," I repeated.

After hearing me repeat the name, Leslie burst out laughing. I smiled because I knew why.

"What's so damn funny?" I asked anyway.

"I know you didn't hire a stylist with a country-ass name like Nora. Sounds like she should been basing hair on *Steel Magnolias*. Ain't no client up in your shop gone let her near their head. You wait and see."

Leslie continued to laugh as she grabbed a cheese biscuit out of the basket that the waitress had just delivered to the table. She bit into her biscuit then observed me and laughed again.

"Nora," she repeated the name.

"All right, you are laughing now, but when you see her hair game you gone be tryin' to make an appointment with her. Fuck what her name is, the bitch is bad."

I grinned and took a sip of my Triple Berry cocktail. The flavor rested on my tongue and eased my mind. *Steel Magnolias*: I could not believe she thought of that. Leslie was funny as hell. I swear that sounded just like something Rochelle would say.

"But that's good. Real talk, I am glad you found some help. Do you think Rochelle gone be out for a while?"

There was the question that I did not want to be asked. I took another sip before answering because, to be honest, I was unsure of what to say.

"For now I'm going to say yes, but I really do not know. She can come back whenever she is ready to come back."

Leslie shook her head as if she understood. She took a sip of her white wine and then screwed up her jaws real tight before clearing her throat.

"Whew," she breathed. "The first sip always tingles in my throat."

She smiled as her face relaxed and she raised the glass again for her next taste.

"I'm thinking about going out of town this weekend," she announced with a grin so wide that all of her teeth showed.

"Where are you going?"

"Chicago. My boo invited me out so I thought, why not." She shrugged her shoulders. "I could use a few days away from Detroit."

I savored the flavor of the sauce from my Cajun chicken pasta in my mouth and agreed, "I guess it wouldn't hurt, but please bring me back a good bottle of wine or somethin' Chicago style."

"Hmmm, I'll think about it. I would hate to be the one to blame for your turning into an alcoholic," she teased.

After a good lunch and some laughter, I jumped back in the Bentley and sped off toward my family's condo for a visit. I dropped by the bank and picked up five thousand for Ma to put in her pocket. It had been a couple of months since I had given her cash and she hardly ever asked for anything. She still worked, but I paid all the bills at the condo. Nevertheless, I still liked to throw her and Monica cash often. Monica was straight for a minute. I had given her eight thousand two months ago, so she was still good. Shopping was her only habit, which I gladly sponsored because she deserved it. Regardless of some of the choices she made, she was a good kid. She did good in school and was an awesome mom to Imani.

"Hey, Ma." I kissed her on the cheek.

"Hey, what brings you by at this time of day? Why you ain't at the salon? I thought you were short a stylist with Rochelle being out?" Her concern was genuine.

"Oh, I got that covered. I told you that I was thinking about hiring someone else permanently, and I did. That pressure is off my ever so heavy shoulders." I pounced down on the sofa like I was tired.

"That's good. I need to make me an appointment." She rubbed her silky hair.

"You know we got you. Just make the appointment, Ma."

"I will as soon as I have some free time. I've been so busy lately."

"Where's Dad at?" I asked.

It felt good to be able to say that.

"He left about an hour ago. He said he had to make some runs and get his hair cut. This morning we went out car shopping and he copped a cream-colored 2014 Lexus IS F. It's cute, too."

"For real?" I smiled, but instantly started to worry. They knew how it worked. But I wanted to be certain. "How much cash did he drop down?"

Anytime you spent over ten thousand, the dealership had to report it to the IRS, and with Dad being on probation and having no job that paid that type of money, that could cause trouble he was not looking for, especially with him being an ex-dealer.

"It's cool, don't worry. We put the car in my name and he only put down eight thousand," Ma explained.

"Cool. I was about to get worried."

"No, we know the deal. He really appreciates Hood hooking him up. I'm glad he was able to get that car. I think it raised his spirits. You know he's used to having nice things."

"I know, and Hood doesn't mind helping out. You know how he is when it comes to our family. We just want Dad keep his nose clean so that we can get through this."

"I feel the same way. He has been talking about maybe opening up a car detail shop once he's off probation."

"That would be a good idea, Ma. We just got to get through this and we got him. Giving him money for a detail shop is nothin'."

I loved hearing about his ideas. The way I saw it, him having a positive plan showed his commitment to doing the right thing. It also made it that much more real that he was out of prison and at home. I was still in disbelief that he was free, and deep down I was afraid, because I knew that the simplest criminal act could land him back in the same place he just came from— this time possibly for life. Just thinking about that forced tears to my eyes and intense beating of my heart.

Chapter 8

I was groggy as hell standing in the kitchen, and Hood was to blame. We had stayed up late the night before playing dominos. I beat him six games straight and he would not give up. He knew I was the dominos champion in the house, not to mention he had been taking tequila shots all night. I took advantage of that. In the end, the only thing that pried him from the table was my soft lips. Now I was paying for it. I had to be up early, but all I wanted to do was go get back in bed.

Hood was wide awake, though. Only he could take tequila shots straight and wake up energized and ready to hustle. Not me. I was groggy and wished I was in bed instead of listening to Hood handle business.

"Just set up the meeting for later today. No

later than five, I have other shit on my plate tonight. I know that—" Hood paused. "I don't give a fuck."

Hood boasted on his cell, so I knew he was talking to Lonzo. I was loading the last few dishes in the dishwasher from breakfast. I had to be at the salon early. One of my clients was getting married and I had to get her head beat for the wedding. She was already a nervous wreck, so I did not want to be late. Plus my new stylist, Nora, was starting today and I had to show her around and introduce her to everyone.

"Look, I got to run over to the Brewster for about an hour, hit me up with the time. Nigga, don't botch this. And let her know that this shit is urgent. A'ight."

The word "her" caught my attention. Who the hell was "her"? I shut the dishwasher and headed for Hood just as he ended the call.

"So who is 'her'? You meetin' with a chick?"

"Yeah, I gotta meet with that Quad bitch. You know, the one runnin' that new squad."

I shook my head. I knew who he was talking about. I remembered Lonzo mentioning her a few weeks back. But I still didn't understand why Hood had to meet with her. I guess that question was written on my face, so without any more questions he explained.

"Them li'l niggas she got on her squad runnin' around the city reckless and actin' wild. They tried that shit on one of my blocks last night and my guys killed two of them. So I'm going to meet with her before shit gets any crazier. If I don't, the streets about to be stupid ignorant."

"Who all going with you to meet with her?"

"Lonzo and a couple of my beasts."

That I understood. You always took your best because you never knew how things would go down. Situations could go from calm to war in a matter of seconds. You just had to be prepared. I still could not believe that a bitch was in charge of a squad. That was a first in Detroit. We had some ruthless chicks around the city, but none took on a squad. Clearly, she was not from around here.

"Okay, but don't you be smilin' and talkin' all sweet to that female."

Grabbing me into a bear hug, he whispered in my ear sweetly, "Why, are you jealous?"

I looked up at him and smiled. "No, but I will pop a cap in a bitch quick about my husband. You tell her that."

We both started laughing as our lips locked in a deep, passionate kiss.

"Now that is what's up," Hood said as we came up for air.

"Okay, I have to get going. I can't be late for Nesa's hair or she gone be trippin'. She already a nervous wreck and thinking everything gone go-wrong."

"Yeah, well, wish them well for me."

"No doubt I will. And you keep your head today, be cool and careful."

"No worries, babe. I will hit you later." He reached down and gave me one last kiss on the lips before I turned and reached for my keys.

When I arrived at the salon, Trina and Pam were standing around chopping it up. I asked Pam if she had contacted all of Rochelle's clients to let them know of the change. As I expected, she had.

"Good, good. So from now on, Nora will take them, and Trina, you and I can take on a few."

"That's cool, we will do what we got to."

"Nora has two scheduled already this morning," Pam informed me.

"Okay, well, she should be here in a minute. I will show her around and take her to her new area. When Nesa gets here, take her on back. Did you bring in the fruit tray and wine, Pam?"

"Girl, please, you know I did. Hell, with the night I had, I can't wait to get a swallow."

"I guess that means Chris came over last night." Trina smiled.

"He sure did." Pam blushed.

Chris was her new boo thang and they were horny for each other like two teenagers. So when he was around they barely ate or drank anything, because only one thing mattered to them: sex.

"Pam, you two are off the chain." I grinned.

"Well, ain't nothin' wrong with it," Trina chimed.

"Don't worry, you gonna meet someone." Pam looked at Trina.

"Well, I don't know about all that, but I'm leaving early today. I got me a little date tonight."

"With who?" I asked.

"Just some guy I met."

"Do tell."

Pam sat down in her chair waiting to be dished the dirt.

"Look, it ain't much to tell right now, but I will tell you all about the date, blow by blow, okay."

I was just about to force the issue when the door flew open and Nora walked in. With smiles on our faces, we jumped into business mode. After reintroducing Nora to Pam and Trina, I showed her around the salon and then left her to prepare for her first client. It felt strange leaving her in Rochelle's booth area. In some ways, I felt like I had abandoned Rochelle. Yeah, Nesa needed to hurry up because I could not wait to open that bottle of wine, either. I needed a drink.

Chapter 9

It was ladies' night out at the club. No men would be tagging along. Monica was geeked that she finally was going to have the fun that she asked for. As we rounded the corner that opened up into the dance floor, we noticed a tall guy standing close to the bar staring at us. We didn't give him a second thought and continued to our destination. Monica followed me, looking around in awe. This was her first time inside this club or any club. Actually, I was proud that this was her first time, because where we come from, in the Brewster, chicks start sneaking in clubs when they are like fifteen, doing everything that the grown people do. But somehow, Monica had missed all of that. I was glad because tonight was new to her and she had something to look forward to. As her older sister, I would introduce her to that experience in a safe, respectable way. Not out acting crazy and taking stupid risks.

We stepped inside our normal VIP area, where Trina and her cousin, Sheila, were already sitting on one of the sofas sipping on margaritas. By the glee on their faces, I knew they were already tipsy.

"What's up, chicas?" I spoke.

"Gettin' it in." Trina raised her glass in my direction and bobbed her head to Ciara's "Body Party."

"What's up, Mya," Sheila spoke.

I knew her from the salon. Trina had brought her through a couple of times. She was really cool. Her life was complicated, though. Her baby's father had run out on her and left her with five kids. She worked hard to take care of them without any government help. I was proud of her; not too many young females stepped up like that. After introducing Sheila to Monica, we headed over to the VIP bar to grab some drinks. Monica was not yet twenty-one, but she did drink. Plus, she was my sister, so no one would dare ID her. When she came over to the house to hang out, I would give her wine or make margaritas. After Dad had first gone to prison, we would sneak into his liquor stash and drink it when Ma was not around. The memory made me blush. Li'l Bo and I would get tipsy and bump into walls. We would laugh until our stomachs ached.

"Mya, this club is nice." Monica stirred the

olive around that was inside her martini before taking a sip.

"I know. Make sure you enjoy yourself." I grinned.

"Trust me, I will," she said as she bit into her olive.

"Hey, bitches!"

I heard Leslie yell as she stepped out of the VIP area. I looked around and spotted her at the bar chatting with some females. They were probably chicks she knew from her block. But I knew she would be hanging with us in VIP. And in no time we had turned up.

We took a seat for a minute after we had been dancing for a minute. Our VIP waiter came over with a bottle of Cristal. As he sat it on ice in front of us, I looked at him long and hard.

"We didn't order this."

"No it was a gift," the waiter spoke up.

He tilted his head a little to the right and pointed. Without another word, the waiter walked away. His finger led us to the tall light-skinned guy that Monica and I saw staring at us earlier as we entered the club. I looked at Monica and she shrugged her shoulders, because neither of us knew who the dude was.

"Well, let's drink up and continue to turn up," Leslie chanted as she reached for the bottle.

The waiter returned with glasses. Before long, we were halfway through the bottle and more krunk than ever. Without being invited, the unknown dude stepped into our VIP area. Normally, I would have checked him, but for some reason I was on chill. He stopped in front of Monica and me looking from one of us to the other.

"Hi, I'm Rich," he said.

I looked at him like I was unimpressed and Monica never said a word. Rich smiled.

"I, ahh, I sent this bottle over as a token of appreciation for attending my club tonight. I'm the owner."

I knew Ripple Turn was getting a new owner because the last owner had sold the place. Apparently, he had cheated on his wife so many times with the girls that ran up through there that she had filed for divorce. The only way she agreed to stay with him and call off the divorce was if he sold the club. But I had no idea who he had sold it to. This dude was corny as hell.

I chuckled because if that was some type of line he had just given for buying the drink, it sucked. And besides, we could care who he was, so why he felt the need to introduce himself was beyond me.

"So did you buy a bottle of Cristal for everyone attending the club tonight?"

With his eyes glued on Monica he replied, "No, this table is special."

I looked from Rich to Monica and, to my surprise, she was blushing and loving the attention that Rich was giving her. I mean, to be honest, dude was fine as hell, but he could step out of my sister's face. I didn't care who he was, but this was not that. The mug on my face said just that.

"Well, you ladies enjoy your bottle and have a good night."

I was glad to see his corny ass walking away.

"Hmmm, he sure had his eyes glued on you, Monica," Leslie commented.

"Ummm, no he didn't." Monica took a big swallow of her margarita, polishing off what was left.

"Well, that doesn't matter, because he is too old for Monica," I added.

Monica laughed. She knew my protective instincts had kicked in and she loved to toy with me.

"That is to be determined."

I looked at her and smiled. That girl was every bit of Li'l Bo, a hard head.

After finishing off that bottle of Cristal, not one of us could sit down. We danced until we fell down. When Monica started to nod, I knew it was time to leave. She was not used to how we could party. We were vets, we could go on and on, but it was time to bounce. After tipping the waiter about five hundred, we grabbed our stuff and prepared to leave.

We were almost out of the club when I saw Rochelle sitting at a table near the dance floor. I decide to go over and speak. To be honest, I was shocked to see her out. As I was walking up to her table, I noticed this guy that I had never seen before sitting with her. He had his face so close to hers that I just knew he was about to kiss her.

I stepped into their space. "Hey, Rochelle," I spoke.

"Hey, Mya." She smiled. I had not seen her smile in so long that I blinked.

"I didn't know you would be out tonight."

Not that she told me anything anymore. I never heard a word from her.

"I guess I didn't either, but my new friend here, Kalil, asked me out. So here I am. Kalil, this is my girl, Mrs. Mya."

Rochelle's words were slurred and her eyes looked dilated; she just did not look right. Kalil looked at me and spoke, but I was not interested in speaking back. I did not know him but everything about him read hustler and loser. He reminded me of Dontae, one of Rochelle's previous loser boyfriends. One thing I knew for sure, Rochelle did not need him in her life at this point. I had no idea where she found these guys.

Her eyes met Monica for the first time. "Oh, hey, Monica, what you doing in the club?"

"Just hanging out with Mya," Monica managed. The look on her face showed that she was worried about Rochelle, but she was under the influence of the drinks, so she could not respond.

"Ummm, Rochelle, you ready to go home? I could drop you off," I offered.

"Oh, no, I'm cool. Kalil gone make sure I get home. I'm good."

That didn't surprise me at all. I figured she would say that. But I wasn't ready to give up.

"Are you sure? It won't be a problem," I reassured her.

"Look, li'l momma, I got this," Kalil had the nerve to say.

How dare that nigga address me. I swung my head around to Kalil. Clearly, he had me fucked up. "My name is Mya." I rolled my eyes at him so hard it hurt. If she wanted to ride with his lame ass, I did not care. "Rochelle, I'll talk to you later."

With nothing else to say, I continued out of the club. I almost spit in that nigga's face, calling me li'l momma. He don't know me like that.

Chapter 10

It had been a couple of days since Hood had that meeting with Quad. I had been so busy that I forgot to ask him how it went. When I left for the salon this morning, he was asleep so he stopped by the salon just to kiss me good morning. I loved when he did things like that, to me that was romantic. Our connection was just as tight as when we first got together.

"You have to stop waking up and leaving like that. I miss you even more when you do that," Hood said, hugging me so tight that I could not breathe.

"Babe, you gone squeeze me to death," I joked.

"I'm sorry. I just missed you. I had to have you in my arms ASAP."

Before he was done, he had kissed my entire

face. I was blushing like a girl who had just fallen in love. In fact, that was how I felt. That's how I always felt when it came to Hood. He always made me number one.

"So how did the meeting go the other day with Quad?"

"It went okay. I told her straight up to get that shit under control or we gone have a problem. And they don't want it."

Hood was straight up like that. His heart was big, but his killing mentality was bigger. The streets knew that he would bring the heat.

"I ran into Rochelle at the club the other night and she was with this guy called Kalil. You ever heard of a dude who goes by Kalil in the streets? He looks just like a hustler, his demeanor and all."

I had not told Hood before about seeing them in the club. I had forgotten all about it with me being so busy. But I woke up with Rochelle on my mind so I thought this was a good time to ask about Kalil.

"If he is who I think, he is a new cocaine dealer to the area. Petty shit, nothin' major, but he heated in the streets."

Those were the exact words that I did not want to hear.

"And for real, for real you need to see what's up with Rochelle, because Kalil is in the fast lane."

"Damn, babe, what I am going to do? Right now Rochelle ain't Rochelle. I don't know what to do."

"Look, babe, you will figure out something."

Hood tried to sound convincing, but I was not so convinced at that exact moment.

"Where Lester at?" Hood looked around like he expected to see him walk in.

"I don't know, he ain't been comin' in." I sighed, frustrated thinking about Rochelle.

Nora walked in. "Oh, I'm sorry, I can come back," she apologized when she saw Hood.

"No it's cool, come on in. This is my husband, Hood. Hood, this Nora, the new stylist."

"What's up?" Hood spoke.

"Hi." Nora reached out to shake Hood's hand. "Mya, I'll come back." Nora walked away this time before I could protest.

"I'm out. Got make these stops." Hood bent down and kissed me on the lips. "Aye, meet me tonight at Flat Bar and Grill. I got a taste for stir-fry."

"It's a date." I smiled. He knew how much I loved stir-fry.

As Hood exited, I bounced down in my chair and my mind pondered over Rochelle. I grabbed my cell phone and hit Rochelle. It went straight to her voicemail, so I left a message.

Chapter 11

It was Saturday and I was in my cleaning mood. I woke with the past on my mind. I remembered how my mom would get us all up on a Saturday morning and have us all cleaning. Li'l Bo, Monica, and I would argue over who should be doing what, even though Ma had already given us instructions. By the time Momma put on some music, like Evelyn "Champagne" King, we would all be grooving to the beat and in good spirits. Dad would be out doing his thing making the money. All we had to do was not worry about anything. Had I known then that his life would bring our family to our knees, I would have begged him to stop. But now, in some ways, we have had a second chance.

So this morning with those thoughts on my

mind, I turned on some Evelyn "Champagne" King and started cleaning. I was running around with a DustBuster singing along with Evelyn's "Betcha She Don't Love You" just as the doorbell rang. I strolled over to open the door. I knew it was Monica because she had called first thing, saying she would be stopping by for minute. As I swung the door open I expected to see her and Imani, but she was alone.

"Hey, sis, where Imani?"

"Dad and Ma have her. They taking her to Chuck E. Cheese today, so I'm free to do whatever."

"Ain't nothin' wrong with being free, but I wanted to see my niece," I pouted.

"Next time, sis."

She stepped inside looking all cute, rocking a chevron-striped sleeveless maxi dress with a pair of black Guess T-strap sandals with shiny things around the ankle and zipper up the back.

"I'm feelin' that outfit," I commented.

"Thanks, and it is comfortable, too."

"I like them maxi dresses, too. I picked up two about a month ago. I'ma have to slide into one." I made a mental note to do just that.

"Dang, I see you jamming, and you taking it way back."

"I know, right. You remember those days."

"Yeah, brings back memories."

Monica smiled and started moving her hips and snapping her fingers. I joined her as we clowned around for a minute. Finally out of breath, we started laughing. I headed over to the entertainment system and turned down the music.

"Yo, and what's up with the cleaning outfit?" Monica joked at the apron and the bandana I had tied around my head. "If you gotta look like that, you need to think about getting a maid to help you clean up this mansion."

"No, thanks. I don't need a maid when I can do it myself."

"If you say so. Is Hood here?"

"No, he left already. Shit been crazy for him lately. These niggas want to see him act up."

"Speaking of niggas, I saw Rochelle last night at CVS with that same dude from the club. What's up with her?"

"I don't know. I can't even catch up with her. She don't return my calls or shit. Did you talk with her?"

Monica shook her head no.

"She seemed strange like she did that night at the club, not like her usual self at all. I called her name but I guess she didn't hear me." She shrugged her shoulders and twisted the corners of her mouth.

"Damn, I need to catch up with her."

Monica and I both got silent for a while. I felt Monica staring at me as I had my head down.

"Look, forget all that. I came by here to chat it up about something. I got to tell you something and I'm telling you this so you won't hear it nowhere else and get pissed at me."

The scowl on my face told her to spit it out. I hate beating around the bush.

"Monica, would you spit it out. Damn, I ain't gettin' no younger."

Monica cast her eyes down without looking at me. Clearly, this news was going to blow my mind. "I'm going out on a date with Rich."

Rich? I searched for the name in my head, but it was not ringing a bell. "Who is Rich?"

Monica looked at me strangely until she realized that I really didn't know him.

"Rich, the guy from the club. Cristal . . . remember?" She paused as if I was slow.

And suddenly it clicked. "Oh, hell no! He is too old for you, Monica!" My eyes stretched big.

"No, Mya, he is not too old for me, and so what if he is. I'm going." She folded her arms ready to argue her case.

I knew she was in her stubborn mode and I really didn't feel like arguing with her. "How did this come about?"

A grin spread across Monica's face from ear to ear. "We ran into each other at Starbucks and he asked me out."

"Hmmph," I grunted. "That's it."

"Mya, don't be like that. He seems like a nice guy."

"What do you mean 'he seems nice'? You don't even know that old-ass dude."

"Mya, stop it with the old crap, he can't be no more than five years older than me. Either way he's worth finding out."

"Whatever. I guess since it's just a date."

"Really, you are okay with it?" Monica jumped up and hugged me.

"Get off me, you're messing up my cleaning mode." I smiled.

I knew how much my support meant to Monica, but to be honest, I didn't see any good coming out of this. But I would let it go for now. I had to let her make her own decisions. Sometimes.

Chapter 12

Looking in the mirror, I decided that I looked a mess. My eyes were red and I had a headache from hell. I needed to do something to get rid of the harsh banging. I popped two extra-strength Excedrin into my mouth and jumped into the shower. The hot shower did me justice; I dried off and got dressed. When I went downstairs to the kitchen, I drank a glass of orange juice, kissed Hood good-bye, and rolled out. Now my head was feeling one hundred percent better, but after looking at my face in the rearview mirror, I decided I needed a pick-me-up. And a little mascara would do just that. I never wore a lot of makeup; in fact, most times I didn't because I didn't need it. It was times like these that I felt like it would help, so I kept some at the salon or a tube in my purse just for that. After applying my mascara, I went to work. My appointments all arrived right on schedule.

"Hey, Trina," I spoke as she stepped in my area at the salon. I had already knocked out three heads and was looking forward to grabbing something to eat soon.

"Hey." Trina stretched and yawned. "I just finished a sew-in that got me tired as hell."

"I feel your pain. I'm about ready for a nap myself," I replied as I sat down in my chair.

"So how is Nora working out? I'm always so busy that I hardly ever get to check in on her."

"She's doing good. All the customers love her work," I said proudly.

"That's good." Trina smiled.

"Hey ladies." Dad strolled in with his paint clothes on.

Trina and I both spoke. I had not seen him all morning, but clearly, he had been working hard, because he was covered in paint from head to toe.

"How is it going down there?" I inquired about the basement.

"It is coming along just fine. Right now, I'm a little hungry and I think I'ma head out to lunch."

"Okay, Dad, I'll see you later."

"Yeah, see you later, Lester," Trina said.

"Mya, I love having him around. You did not tell me your dad was funny as hell," Trina said after he walked out of the room. "Shit, he could have his own comedy spot."

I chuckled, thinking about some of the jokes that he told. He was funny. "I know he is, he told us jokes all the time when we were coming up. My brother Li'l Bo could be funny just like him."

While I was talking to Trina, I remembered that she never told me what happened with her date. So I decided to get in her business and ask her about it.

"I've been meaning to ask, how was your date? I thought we were supposed to be hearing the blow-by-blow action."

Trina started laughing. "Girl, it was a joke! He kept texting on his phone the whole time like a teenager. Then, when we got ready to leave the restaurant, there was a pregnant girl standing outside slicing his tires, talkin' about she was his wife."

My mouth flew open. "Hell no, this nigga is married?"

We both burst out laughing.

"I almost ran his ass over tryin' to get out that parking lot. Do you know he gone yell 'yo Trina, can I call you later.' I screamed out my window as I burned rubber, 'Hell no, my phone just got disconnected.'"

Trina and I both were bent over laughing and talking about that dude. As we simmered down, we heard loud talking, then Pam ran in.

"Mya, you need to come up here and talk to Rochelle, she trippin'."

I followed Rochelle's loud voice to her booth area, where she was all up in Nora's face yelling at her for working in her space. Nora was calmly trying to explain, but Rochelle was throwing her hands up and getting all in her space.

I grabbed Rochelle, pulled her out of Nora's face, and told her to calm down. Rochelle turned to me yelling, "Who is this bitch and why is she working in my area?"

"Rochelle, it is only temporary. Nora is a stylist here and the power isn't working in her area right now."

Rochelle continued to yell and curse while she snatched her equipment and threw things. She seemed so enraged I stepped back. As I wondered what she might do next, Big Nick appeared out of nowhere.

"What's going on?" Big Nick asked.

"Nothing. I have it under control," I lied.

Next, Dad stepped in the room and looked from Rochelle to me. "Mya, what's going on?" He looked at Rochelle then back at me, but I did not have an answer.

"She's just upset. She will be all right in a minute."

Dad walked over and started talking to Rochelle, but she wasn't hearing him or anyone else. Nora, Trina, and Pam stepped out at my request.

"Dad, just let me handle it. I got it," I assured him. I wanted to speak with Rochelle alone.

Reluctantly he agreed. "All right. I am going to step out with Big Nick for a minute." He was cradling a McDonald's bag in his hand.

"Rochelle, why you acting like this? You haven't been yourself lately. What can I do to help? This is still your area and when you are better you can come back to it. Let me help you. Just tell me how I can help," I all but begged.

Instead of saying anything to me, Rochelle threw most of her hot irons and a few other things in a bag and stormed out, pissed. Again, I had not reached her. I was still at square one. And for some reason, I felt like this was only the beginning.

Chapter 13

My head was still messed up from the earlier scene with Rochelle. I was lost. I hoped meeting up with Hood would help. Normally, when I was upset or having problems, he could cool me down and give me reassurance. It was simple, he had my back just like I had his, not only physically, but emotionally, too. I was a strong believer that a relationship needed that at the core to sustain. Our relationship was stronger than any issue and I didn't see anything tearing it apart. And whatever tried would have a helluva time.

I pulled into the restaurant and saw that the parking lot was packed. I knew the crowd would be thick inside. I really didn't feel like being around a lot of people, but it was what it was. I hopped out of my Mercedes and strolled inside.

I told the hostess that I was with a party of two and she informed me that Hood was already there and waiting for me. I fell in line behind the waitress as she led the way.

Hood stood up as he saw me approach. Reaching out, he hugged and kissed me. That was exactly what I needed, his comfort. "Hey, babe." He spoke as I sat down across from him in the booth. The weary look on my face showed automatically. I could not hide it and there was no faking how I felt.

"What's going on?" He looked me in the eyes with concern.

Tears burned my eye sockets. I cast my eyes down for just a second. I hated to be the downer of our meal. But one thing that I knew for sure was that he wanted to be there for me.

"I don't know. Rochelle showed up at the salon today trippin'. I'm talking about throwing things and yelling and she wouldn't listen to no one, including my dad. Poor Nora—she cursed that girl out so bad, had I not pulled her back, she might have hit her."

The scene played back in my head. Rochelle had acted awful.

"For real." Hood was surprised. "Damn, babe, but it's just like I said before, you got to give her time. She is acting out because of Todd's death, that's all."

"I know, but I have never seen Rochelle behave this way, especially with me. She treats me like a complete stranger. "

Tears ran down my face as my emotions got the best of me. I wanted to be in control of them right now but I could not. It was just so much; Rochelle was not even the whole issue.

I laid it all out. "Not only that, I think Dad is spending too much time with Big Nick. I mean I know they are like best friends and Big Nick has been there for all of us. I turned to him for help when I couldn't trust or turn to anyone else. But I am worried. Big Nick is popping up at the shop all the time and picking him up lately. Why does he need to pick him up when Dad has his own car? A damn good car at that—he can drive. I'm telling you, Hood, something is just strange." I was convinced and I did not like the feeling.

"Babe, you need to calm down. You got too much on your mind when it comes to Rochelle and your dad. You need to fall back a bit. As for your dad, I'll check up on him and make sure he's straight. But you have to promise me that you will stop worrying. A'ight."

This time it was Hood with the worried look. The last thing I wanted to do was stress him out because I knew how much he had on his plate. So I promised him that I would chill or at least I would do my best to.

Chapter 14

Rochelle was on my mind all night. Every dream I had involved her but none were clear. Matter of fact, I don't believe I clearly saw her face once. I tossed and turned with restlessness; the feeling was unbearable. I wanted to be free from it, but in my sleep there seemed to be no way out. I felt like I was in a maze. The relief I would get was if my eyes were opened, and even though I was dreaming, I believed that. Eventually, but not soon enough, I woke up.

When I finally woke up, I was a bit shaken from anxiety, so after jumping in the shower and throwing on some clothes, I decided to make my first stop at Mrs. Wynita's house. My stomach growled from hunger but the uneasiness in my throat would not allow me to eat. The only thing that would make me feel better at this point would be seeing Mrs. Wynita and Tiny.

Mrs. Wynita smiled when she opened the door, but it didn't hide the despair that was all over her face. I remembered her acting crazy when Rochelle and I would stroll up in the house late. Or the fits she would throw over Rochelle not going to church. Those thoughts warmed me as I reached out and gave her a much-needed hug. Soon after that, Tiny came from the back of the house. She was so happy to see me that she jumped up into my arms. I remembered how precious she was as a baby and how she would hold up her arms to be picked up. She was so adorable and just as cute today.

"Auntie, Auntie, I missed you. Did you come to take me home? I miss Mommy. And Granny says I can't stay with her. We didn't even go see her."

Hearing her say that broke my heart in two. Tiny was no longer a baby; she understood what was going on. How much longer could we go without telling her the truth? She would want to know why she could not see Rochelle.

"No, sweetheart, we can't go see her right now." Mrs. Wynita held a fake smile on her face; she knew what I was thinking. "But I did come to see you. I have missed you soooo much." I hugged her tight. Mrs. Wynita continued to smile at us as she turned around and closed the door behind me. Tiny released her grip on me and headed over to sit down in front of the television.

"How have you been, Mrs. Wynita?" I turned to face her.

The tears were stinging at her eyes. She wasn't really used to seeing me without seeing Rochelle. We were always together, two peas in a pod.

"I've been okay. Just working and taking care of Tiny. I had to change my schedule up a little bit so that I can get her back and forth to school. But it's working out fine."

"If you were having trouble getting her back and forth to school, why didn't you call me? I could have helped out." I was hurt that she had not called me for help.

"No, it's fine. I took care of it. I know you have the salon to worry about and I know you are down a stylist." She waved her hand. "I didn't want to bother you with this."

"Mrs. Wynita, none of that matters. If you ever need me, I'm just a phone call away. I have help at the salon. I'm not doing it alone so I'm always available to help you. Besides, I hired a new stylist, so that is taken care of. You and Tiny are family, and family comes first. Okay? Please don't count me out."

"All right," she finally agreed.

Mrs. Wynita was independent: she did not like to depend on anyone. I was starting to believe that was a genetic trait for African American women, including myself. Hood had a hard time getting me to stop being so independent. I still struggled with that.

"Come on let's have a cappuccino." She grinned. She was happy to have me there. "Rochelle brought me this machine last Christmas. I hardly ever use it. Tiny, I'll fix you some hot chocolate and bring it to you."

"Thanks, Granny."

Tiny never took her eyes off the television, she and Imani alike were television fans. She was watching the Alvin and the Chipmunks movie and you could tell that it had her undivided attention.

Mrs. Wynita turned on the cappuccino machine. I grabbed a chair at the table and sat down. Now my mouth was watering for a cappuccino. The knot in my throat had gone away. Seeing them had been as therapeutic as I thought it would be.

"So have you met Rochelle's new boyfriend? What's his name, Kalil?"

The words came off Mrs. Wynita's tongue sour. That told me everything that I needed to know. She did not approve of him. At least I was not the only one who knew he was not in Rochelle's best interest.

"Yeah, I've seen him around. She introduced us. But only as a friend, never a boyfriend." I remembered the night she introduced him very vividly.

"Oh, that's her man all right. She made that clear to me the other day when I went by there." Mrs. Wynita was matter-of-fact in her words.

"So you went to her house?"

"Umm hmm. I went by to pick up some more clothes for Tiny, since I couldn't get her to pick up the phone." I knew that feeling of her not answering calls all too well. "Anyway, he answered the door like it's his house or something. He had all his so-called boys over there laying all around the living room. And the house looked like the junkyard down at the city dump. Shit was everywhere. I was so disgusted, and you know me, I couldn't hold back. I don't care who was there. I went off cursing and everybody started to scramble and clear out. Lord help me, had I had a gun I probably would have started shooting, I was so angry. So I ask her what is going on and she looked at me all strange, almost like she was in some type of zone, like she couldn't understand. She's just not herself at all anymore. She behaves very differently."

I could hear the shakiness in Mrs. Wynita's voice. She was becoming emotional but she concealed it well.

"It has been the same for me when I try to talk with her. I just can't seem to connect with her anymore. I have tried several times."

I decided to leave out what had happened at the salon the day before. Emotionally, I didn't know if Mrs. Wynita was ready for that. The last thing I wanted to do was give her another reason to stress.

"Do you know she had the nerve to ask me if Tiny could spend the night with her? She asked me that with all them damn weirdoes laying around up in there. I told her over my dead body and until she get her life back together, she can forget about Tiny. And I meant that. She will never see Tiny again if she don't straighten up and fly right. I raised her better. And I will not . . ." She paused as she got emotional. Placing her hand over her mouth, she tried to calm herself so that she could finish what she had to say. Patiently I waited. "I will not have my grandchild around such filth and trash. That environment ain't safe and I don't trust that damn Kalil as far as I can throw that heathen," she spat after she had gathered her composure again.

"Me neither," I agreed.

I laughed inside at the way she described Kalil as a heathen. I wasn't exactly sure what heathen meant, but I knew it was ratchet and she meant those words to be harsh. Mrs. Wynita handed me a mug full of hot cappuccino. I licked my lips at the creamy concoction as I wrapped my hands around the mug. The warm feeling of the cup calmed me. I stayed for a while and talked with Mrs. Wynita. We both agreed that we would not give up on Rochelle, we loved her too much. I could not wait until the day that I could have a rational conversation with my best friend again while she smoked a Newport.

Chapter 15

Weeks had gone by and I had not heard a word from Rochelle. All of my calls went unanswered and messages were not returned. I had been by the apartment and banged on the door, still with no response. At some point, she had her locks changed, because I could no longer use my key. I was at my wits' end. Hood told me that word on the streets was that Rochelle had moved in with Kalil. Just hearing that made my blood boil. Why she would move in with him was completely beyond my comprehension. I wanted to physically harm Kalil; in some ways I blamed him for some of Rochelle's behavior. Why couldn't he just stay away from Rochelle? There were a thousand chicks in Detroit looking to come up with a dope boy and the only one he could seem to find was Rochelle. Right now she was too vulnerable; there was not one rational bone in her body. Hurt was the only thing that she was thinking with.

———◉———

I reached over and grabbed my buzzing cell phone. "What's up, Leslie?"

I really didn't feel up to talking, but what the heck. It had been a minute since I spoke with her anyway. I couldn't dodge her forever. Not that I was trying to dodge her on some shady moves. I had just not been in the mood.

"You been MIA since I been back in town. Thought I would catch up to you. What's good in the D?" she asked, referring to Detroit. I could tell that she was hype and ready to chat.

"Working and chillin', trying to maintain." My tone was low-spirited because that was exactly how I felt at the time.

"I hear you. Me too."

I knew she could not wait to spill the fun about her trip so I decided not to waste any more time and ask.

"So how was Vegas?"

Maybe hearing about her trip would lift my spirits. She had recently gone to Vegas with her guy. Come to think of it, they were always traveling out of town lately. Almost every other weekend she was somewhere different. She was really feeling him. I was happy for her.

"Girl, we turned up. Vegas ain't the same since we left. I had so much fun, I can't wait to go back."

"I figured that. I swear I keep hearing that

from everybody who's been so far. Hood and I need to take a trip out there," I suggested just as my phone started to beep. Looking at the screen, I saw it was Ma trying to call.

"Aye, look, I gotta call comin' in. I'ma hit you back."

"Okay, I will call you later," Leslie said before I ended the call.

"Mya," Ma yelled my name and I instantly knew something was up.

"Hey, Ma, what's up?" I could hear her remove the phone from her mouth as she was fussing.

"Ma," I yelled to get her attention.

"Mya, Monica over here talking about she's moving out. She done went crazy."

"Ma, we already discussed this but she is going to wait. I forgot to tell you about it, that's all."

"No, she is moving out now. I'm talking right now."

Now I was confused.

"Okay, what is going on?" I wanted to know.

Ma kept yelling at Monica so I knew I would never get anywhere over the phone. I was trying to get her attention, but it sounded like she had laid the phone down.

"Ma, calm down. I will be there in a minute," I yelled through the phone.

I don't know if she heard me or not but I ended the call. After throwing on a pair of sweats and some Jays, I grabbed the keys to the Escalade and headed out the door. That's how my day was starting out—drama.

When I got there I found Imani lying on the living room couch watching television. And just as Ma had said, Monica was in her room packing suitcases and a few boxes. Ma was standing in the doorway yelling at her.

Calmly, I sidestepped past Ma into the room. Asking her to move was out of the question. "Monica, what is going on? Where are you going?" I pointed at her luggage.

To my surprise and horror, she said, "I'm movin' in with Rich." I blinked twice; it was uncontrolled. Shock was fast becoming a part of my life and I was not okay with it.

I was certain that she had lost her mind because she barely knew this fucking dude. Clearly, she was tripping or I was hard of hearing. Maybe I was tripping; if not, I was about to.

"Movin' in with him? You only have been on one date with him."

I gave her a look that said this was ridiculous. Maybe we were being punked.

Without missing a beat, folding clothes into her suitcase, she corrected me. "No, we have been kickin' it for weeks and we decided—" I cut her off.

This girl thought she was grown for real. But that was bullshit to me. "You decided . . . you decided what?"

It was clear now that I was pissed. Monica knew I was not the one to upset, because I could be crazy as hell.

"Yes, Mya . . ." She stopped and looked at me for a second. She was not going to back down. "We decided that we should move in together."

She was matter-of-fact. I hated it when she tried to force my hand.

Ma sighed loudly with frustration. "See, Mya, I told you." Ma looked at me then back to Monica. "You are making a huge mistake." She shook her finger at Monica. "And what about Imani?" That was a good question. I wondered if she had considered Imani or was it all about her love for Rich, a guy she didn't even know.

"She is going with me and she is going to be fine." Monica continued to pack. She had it all figured out. "Besides, she likes Rich."

"Wait, so you have been takin' her around him?" I asked in disbelief. I could not believe her. Taking my niece around some guy that she's only known for ten damn minutes.

"Yes. We have done things together a few times." She said it as though it was normal. Who was she right now?

I looked at her like she was crazy. The next words out of my mouth were going to be reckless if I did not calm down. I took a deep breath and tried to count to fifty. Rochelle's words about me being too protective crossed my mind. I had to choose what I said carefully. Arguing was not the best way to handle a situation like this.

Ma was frustrated. She called my name and I knew she wanted me to say something to change Monica's mind. But anything I said would only makes things worse.

"Mya, say something," Ma urged. She wanted results now.

The problem was that the only result she wanted was for Monica to unpack her clothes and say that she was staying. Unfortunately, at this point, that was not going to happen.

I was at a loss. I looked at Monica, who was still packing, and I saw my sister as a woman and not a child. I turn to Ma. "She grown, ain't nothin' else I can say." I was done.

Those words slowed Monica's hands. She turned and looked at Ma, whose face was covered with wet tears. Ma's tears hurt Monica. Monica was always the one who had worried most about Ma when she had been in the streets on drugs. It was Monica who couldn't get any sleep when she didn't come home. Now the shoe was on the other foot. Monica was a grown woman and Ma didn't want her to move out.

"Besides, Ma, with me gone, you and Dad can have the house alone."

Monica tried to reason, but it would take time for Ma to understand. It would not happen overnight, regardless of what was said. She would miss Imani terribly; she had helped raise her since birth. I think Imani filled the void that she had for losing Li'l Bo.

Her eyes and heart full of hurt, Ma said, "Your dad ain't never here for us to have this place alone. Hell, with you and Imani gone, I will be here by myself. He too damn busy runnin' the streets. And why is this Rich rushin' you to move in with him? What is the damn hurry? Are you pregnant?"

I was not prepared for that question. I looked at Monica.

"Heck no." Monica grinned. "Don't worry, Ma, I won't be having any more children anytime soon."

"You better not be," I chimed in.

I loved Imani to pieces, but Monica was not ready for any more babies anytime soon. She had goals. Hell, to be honest, Rich was not a part of them, but what could we do but move on? This conversation was done and I was literally drained.

"I'm out." I turned to leave but stopped and looked at Monica. "But that nigga betta know whose sista he fuckin' with. You betta make sure he knows that."

That was all I had to say. She wanted to be grown, she had it. Rochelle helped me understand that sometimes you just have to let people experience life and grow up. It hurt, but I had to. Hopefully, Ma would get over it soon, but at this point what choice did she have?

I needed to find out what Dad's fucking problem was, though. He was never around when he needed to be. Those fucking streets were constantly eating people alive and he understood that better than most. So why couldn't he stay out of them?

Chapter 16

I knew just where to my find old Daddy Dearest. I headed straight to Big Nick's crib. He would be there if he was anywhere. Those two ran the streets together night and day; that had not changed. Once inside his building, I went up to the clerk and gave her the information needed to get to his penthouse suite. They were familiar with me so it was not hard. After one call, Big Nick agreed to let them bring me up.

As soon as Big Nick swung the door open, I marched in.

"Where is he?"

Before Big Nick could say a word, I saw my dad chilling, cradling a glass of cognac, one of his favorite drinks. I wanted it to be no mistake that I was pissed.

"What are you doing? Why are you here and your daughter and granddaughter are at home moving out to live with some smooth talkin' ass nigga?"

For some reason as I fussed, my eyes left Dad and gazed at the floor, which was covered with guns and pounds of cocaine. The sight caused me to stumble back in shock.

Slowly my eyes roamed from Big Nick to my father. Dad saw the worry all over my face and stood up.

"Mya, sweetheart, it is not what you think," he tried to explain. He reached out to touch me but I backed up and threw up my right hand to break contact.

"I think I should leave" were the only words that crept out of my mouth.

I was losing him again. It would not be long before he was back behind bars. I was sure of it. I backed all the way up to the door. All the while Big Nick and Dad were chanting different things at me and trying to convince me to stay. But it was like I was in a movie moving in slow motion with no sound. I could hear nothing they said.

When I finally reached the door, I turned around and walked out without saying a word. I rushed to the elevator, where the waiting attendant took me down to the lobby. Once outside, I felt free. My lungs finally opened. I got in my truck, started it, but I didn't leave because I was unable to drive. I sat in a daze for minute. Eventually I pulled off and headed for the interstate.

My cell phone was ringing nonstop. All calls were from Dad. I turned my cell phone off.

When I made it home, Hood was there and that was exactly who I needed. I told him about what happened at Big Nick's house and about Monica moving in with Rich. He was in awe at all the information. He suggested that I get some rest. After drawing me a hot bath and bringing me up a glass of wine, he pulled back the covers and I climbed into bed, closed my eyes, and went to sleep.

Chapter 17

Dad blew my phone up for days before I finally decided to take his call. He may as well have been on block because I ignored the hell out of him. But I couldn't do that forever, so I agreed to meet up with him to talk. I wanted to look him in the face when he told me whatever it was he had to say. I expected him to give me excuses. I just hoped they were the truth.

We sat down to lunch at Panera Bread and discussed the issue over soup and sandwiches. Just as I thought, he promised me that he was not involved in anything illegal. Reluctantly, I decided to let it go. There was just too much going on and it was stressing me out. But I made sure to remind him that it did not matter if he was physically involved, he was on papers, and just being around it was enough to throw him back inside for life.

After lunch with Dad, I headed to the salon because Monica was supposed to be stopping by. I could not wait to chop it with my sister. She had officially been living with Rich for almost two weeks.

"So how do you like playing wifey?" I asked.

"Oh, Mya, ain't nobody playing wifey, but I do like being in my own place."

"Hmmph, well I guess that is a perk."

We laughed as Leslie came in. "Hey, Leslie," Monica spoke.

"What's up? It's been a minute, Monica. What have you been up to?"

"Same thing, school and Imani. Oh, and I moved in with my new man, Rich."

Leslie's eyes popped out of her head. I hadn't had a chance to tell her about Monica and Rich yet. "Wait, Rich from the club?"

"Yep."

"You go, girl. You know he fine as hell and his pockets are fat." Leslie was all hyped. "And why didn't you tell me, Mya? You holdin' out on your girl." Leslie played offended.

"Girl, it slipped my mind. Besides, it's better you heard from Monica anyway," I said as Nora entered the room.

"So, anyway, I was wondering if you ladies wanted to hit the club all on Rich. I'm talkin' VIP, the whole nine. Just like you used to, Mya, but this time you and Hood won't have to spend a dime."

"Shit, I'm cool with that." Leslie wasted no time.

"Yeah, I guess so. Why not?" I shrugged my shoulders.

"You can come too, Nora, we gone party. And, Mya, don't forget to tell Trina and Pam if they want to come out."

"All right, bet."

———◦◈◦———

True to Monica's word, Rich set it out. VIP was on point. Everybody was there. Hood, Lonzo, and their clique were poppin' mad bottles. Drinks were flowing and everyone was having a good time. And of course the DJ was on fire. Rich was smiling ear to ear and being the perfect host. I still was not happy about Monica moving in with him, but it was club night and I wanted to have fun, so I tried not to give him the evil eye. But I did keep an eye on him.

I watched him treat Monica like a queen, showering her with everything she asked for. Leslie was sitting next to me taking small shots of Patrón and she had her eyes wide open. Sometimes she seemed to be in her own zone, like maybe something was bothering her. But she kept a smile on her face, so I assumed that she was cool. She must have noticed Quad heading to another VIP room that was below the one we had reserved, because she leaned into my ear and asked me, "Have you ever met Quad, that new bitch that is running that squad?"

"No."

Without warning, she pointed her out to me. I was shocked, though, because when I pictured this chick running a crew, I pictured this tomboy looking chick. But laying eyes on Quad for the first time it was clear that she was quite the opposite. She looked to be about five foot eight, slim in the waist, and she was rocking a bad-ass shoulder-length wrap. Just as I took her in fully, she gazed upward in my direction and we made eye contact.

The night went on and we continued to turn up, but I started to get tired and decided I was ready to leave. The club would be closing soon and I did not feel like being stuck in the after-the-club traffic. I wanted to make a smooth exit in my thousand-dollar red bottoms. Monica said that she was going to wait on Rich. I almost hated to hear her say that, but it did make sense, since they lived together now. So after telling her good night, I grabbed Hood by the arm and headed out.

As we made our way past the dance floor, I saw Rochelle dancing all wild on Kalil. My heart sped up because I was happy to see her. It had been two months at least since I had last laid eyes on her. Without any hesitation, I walked up to her.

"What's up, Rochelle?" I smiled.

Rochelle stopped dancing and never said one word. We just looked at each other. All of a sudden, she started dancing again like I wasn't even standing there. I turned around and looked at Hood in disbelief. I wondered if he saw what had just happened. He just looked at me. I knew that he, too, was probably at a loss for words. How dare she be so rude to me? I was not a stranger. Stepping up to her, I silently grabbed her by her right arm.

Rochelle forcefully yanked away from my grasp. "What? What, Mya?"

She yelled so loud, you could hear her over the music. People stopped dancing. I looked around slowly as I noticed people watching.

"Why the hell can't you leave me alone? Can't you see a bitch is tryin' to have a good time?" Her rage filled eyes were glued only to me.

I could not believe this was happening. This new Rochelle showed no signs of the old one. She was completely unpredictable. I took a step back, but then without thinking I moved forward. I had to try and I didn't care who saw. "Look, I just wanted to speak. You ain't gotta trip like this."

"Yeah, whatever, just get back before you get me and my new man shot."

I froze. I could not believe those words had left her mouth. That hit me like a ton of bricks.

"What the fuck you just say to me?"

Rochelle stepped toward me. "Bitch, you heard me."

"You know what. Whatever drugs you are on got you saying stupid shit. So I'ma bounce . . . 'cause you trippin' right now." I turned slowly and walked away to leave. But before I could take a step, Rochelle rushed me.

Hood, Kalil, and others that were standing

around pulled Rochelle off me. With tears pouring down my face, I turned to face Rochelle, who was screaming and fighting Kalil. My heart was torn to pieces. It was all clear to me. All of this was my fault. I was the reason for her undoing. My revenge had cost Rochelle dearly.

Chapter 18

"Hey, girl," Trina spoke as I opened the door and let her in. She had stopped by to visit me and watch a movie. She had been unable to make the club the night before because her sisters had a party, so she hung out with them.

"Come on, let's go in the den. I thought we could watch *Baggage Claim*." Hood had found me a good bootleg copy from the screening company, so it would be just like watching it at the theater.

"Oh yeah, I haven't seen that yet."

"Me either, but from what I hear we ain't miss much." I repeated what Monica and Ma had told me. They had gone to the movies to see it and Ma said it was a horrible movie for gullible teenagers. Monica had shrugged her shoulders and agreed. But I decided we could watch it and make our own review.

I had popped some popcorn and grabbed us some Cokes right before she arrived, so we were straight. We sat down and relaxed in the den as I started the movie and the credits rolled.

"So, girl, I ran into Rochelle last night at the club and she tripped out hard on me."

"What happened?"

The last thing I wanted to do was relive it because I was so hurt, but I had to tell Trina. She had known Rochelle for a long time. She also knew how close Rochelle and I were and that there was nothing that could come between us, or at least that was the way it was until recently.

"I don't know. I saw her and I approached her simply to speak and she went crazy on me. She even rushed me like she wanted to fight me."

My eyes beat back the tears as they tried to form in my eye sockets. I had cried all night. I refused to cry today.

"Who? Our Rochelle?" Trina was shocked. "Damn, that is wild. But, Mya, it is going to be okay. Rochelle needs her space for a while so that she can figure some things out. That's all."

"I know, that's what everybody keeps telling me. Stuff is just crazy right now."

I opened my Coke and took a swallow, hoping to melt the knot that was forming in my throat.

"So how is Monica doing since moving in with Rich?"

"She's cool, I guess." I rolled my eyes in the

air. "Every time I see her she seems happy. So for now that is how I'm gone chop it up."

Trina smiled. "That's a good way to look at it. Oh, by the way, we missed the deadline for the hair show."

"I heard, but Reese called me the other day and said that they are probably going to redo them because there were a bunch of mess-ups. So they will let me know."

At this point, I really didn't care about the hair show. I had other things going on that were more important, like the situation with Rochelle. I just was not feeling it, no matter how hard I tried to force it.

"Okay, cool, we might still have a shot, then." Trina seemed relieved. I knew she was excited about doing the hair show because last year had been so successful.

"But I really was not tripping, though. To be honest, if we had missed it, it's because shit just been crazy. And you know I can't do it without Rochelle; it just won't be the same."

"I know. Let's just hope she is better by then, it's still a long way off." Trina shook her head sadly but then smiled. "Shit, we turned up last year, had a fucking ball."

As I remembered the good time we had, I could not hold back my smile. "Yeah, we did."

"But don't worry, all this negativity will pass. We will get back to that. Just you wait and see."

I wanted to be confident, but it was hard. At this point, things just did not look good. Getting comfortable, I leaned back and readied myself for the movie.

Chapter 19

All sadness aside, today was a day for shopping, and I was at one of my favorite stores, Saks. I walked in ready to max out. I welcomed my first glass of champagne with open hands. Leslie had beat me to the store and was already on her second glass.

"Dang, I thought you would never show up," she complained, just as I knew she would.

"Just blame it on the traffic." I sipped.

I set my sights on tops first. Crosby Derek Lam had my attention. I strolled over with Leslie on my trail. I knew she was ready to talk. "These tops are too cute." I had picked out two just that easy.

"I know, I already picked out several for myself," Leslie added.

"How could you start without me?" I thumbed through the selection.

"There is a fix for that and it's called being on time."

"Whatever." I stepped back and sipped out of my glass again.

"So, I have made up my mind to move to Chicago. I will be taking a flight out to go look at some cribs."

I stopped for a minute, looked at her, and sighed. But in the end, I agreed. "I guess if you have thought it through. It can't be all bad. I'm going to hate to see you go, but you have my support."

"Awww, thanks, friend." Leslie smiled and gave me a side hug.

"But if that nigga don't treat you right, you betta drop his ass and I mean quick!"

"Trust me, you know I will," Leslie agreed.

"And are you going to at least let us meet him before you move?"

"Well, I don't know if he will be able to come out anytime soon. Besides, I don't think Hood would approve of him, being close friends with Rob and all."

I kind of understood where she was coming from. But Hood was no fool, he knew she had to eventually move on with her life.

"Hood will be cool. He knows what you have been through and he wants you to be happy." I tried to assure her.

"Speaking of new dudes, you know I heard Kalil be on that white that he slangin'. He krunk off his own shit and I think he got Rochelle on that shit, too. That's why she actin' all crazy."

I'm not sure why Leslie had to bring this up, especially when I was starting to enjoy myself, but that bit of news made my heart drop. Tears formed in my eyes and I was unable to hold them back. Covering my mouth, I started to weep from deep down. Hearing that Rochelle was using drugs took me back to how I used to feel when my mother was getting high.

Leslie reached out, grabbed my drink out of my other hand, and set it down. Wrapping her arms around me, she hugged me for comfort. After a few minutes, I gained my composure and released myself from her embrace. There was a side of me that Leslie knew nothing about, but it was starting to burn inside.

"If he does anything to hurt her, I will make sure that he pays."

The look in my eyes sent a shudder through Leslie. I watched as it passed through her.

Chapter 20

After hearing the news about Rochelle, I couldn't continue shopping. I told Leslie good-bye, jumped in my Mercedes, and headed to my mother's house. I drove all the way there with clouded vision from the many tears that fell. My heart was so heavy it weighed me down. Instead of knocking on the door, I used my key and walked inside. I found Ma sitting on the living room couch watching television. She looked a little surprised to see me.

I wanted to hide the tears but my face was all puffy, so there was no way I could. Ma raised up off the couch with concern. "What's wrong?"

I was unable to control the shaking in my voice. I cried as I told her what Leslie had told me about Rochelle using drugs.

"What can I do to help her?" I needed to know if there was anything I could do to save my friend.

Ma's hurt was lying wide open at this point; she wanted to help me but she had to be honest. "Not much you can do, at least not yet. But that's only because you are one of the last people she wants to hear from right now. Reach out to Wynita, she will listen to her."

I knew that would not help, either. Rochelle was as stubborn as a mule when she was in her right mind. She was a thousand times worse right now.

"Where is Dad at?"

"Hmmph, girl, his ass ain't never home. This house is quiet as hell since Monica and Imani left. You could hear a pin drop."

For some reason, her humor almost made me laugh. I needed that, but at the same time it made me worry about Dad. I decided to keep what I saw at Big Nick's place to myself. The last thing I wanted to do was have Ma worry.

"Maybe we should go out and visit Monica and Imani soon." My tears finally started to dry up.

Smiling, she agreed with me. We sat and talked for a while and she made me a fire-grilled cheese sandwich. On my way to the house, I gave Mrs. Wynita a call and she sounded so happy to hear from me, I had a hard time bringing myself to tell her about Rochelle and the drugs.

She surprised me by saying that Rochelle had come by earlier in the week to see Tiny, but she had not seen or heard from her since. I assured her that everything was going to be okay and that Rochelle would soon be back to her old self. Mrs. Wynita agreed, because she had been praying for her. Now *that* I believed, and it gave me hope.

Chapter 21

Damn, Dad's bullshit was really starting to get on my nerves. Now his PO was calling me looking for him, like I carry him around on my damn hip all day. I gave the PO a bullshit reason about him being out filling applications for another part-time job to go along with the one he worked at the salon. Really, I was in the same position as he was, I had no idea where in the hell Daddy was. Hell, I never knew where he was. He had not been to the salon once in the past week, but everything else kept me so busy that I didn't even have the time to notice.

But today I had to give him a call because his PO sounded pissed; Dad had not showed up to his scheduled appointment. That was a no-no and Dad knew better. I just did not understand what had gotten into him. I scrolled through my contacts, found his name, and hit the call button.

"Hey, Baby Girl," he answered on the second ring.

"Dad, where are you?" I twisted up my nose at his calmness.

"Just out running a couple of errands. Why? What's up?"

"Ahh well, your PO just called. Did you forget that you had an appointment with him today?"

"Shit . . ." He paused. "Yeah, that was today. It kind of slipped my mind. What did you tell him?"

"I told him you were out looking for another job to go along with this one. I didn't know what else to say."

"Well, good lookin' out. I will give him a call and see if I can reschedule."

"Dad, you can't be missing your appointments. That is not cool." I was agitated. To me it seemed like he was being careless for no reason at all. Did the fact that he could be back up in prison mean anything to him?

"Baby Girl, I know. I'm sorry. I don't mean to make you worry."

His apology made me feel a little better, but I was not done.

"What about around here? You haven't been here all week! Not once, Dad. What if they got somebody watching the salon to make sure that you are working? You got to be more careful."

"I hear you, Baby Girl, and I will, I promise." He sounded sincere.

"All right. Well, I will see you tomorrow." I was frustrated as hell and I felt a slight headache coming on.

"Mya." I looked up to see Nora coming in.

"Hey," I spoke back.

"Aye, I'm about to head out and grab me and Pam something for lunch. You want me to bring you something back?"

"What are you getting?" I asked. Before sitting down, I rubbed my forehead, and Nora sensed that something was bothering me.

"A catfish plate." She was watching me. "Are you okay? You seem a little frustrated." She was clearly reading me like a book because I was on edge for real.

"Nah, I'm cool. But you know, it's one of those moments when you could use a drink in the middle of the day."

We both chuckled at the same time. "Yeah I feel you," Nora agreed.

"But other than that, I'm good. Let me grab my purse. I'll take one of those fish plates and get me some extra tartar." I went to grab my purse just as Leslie strolled in. I was surprised to see her. She was supposed to be headed to Chicago.

"What are you doing here? Shouldn't you be at the airport?"

"I'm on my way. I just stopped by to get my eyebrows done. I can't go nowhere looking like a fool. I didn't have time yesterday, so I figured now was as good a time as any to get them done. Good thing your chair is free." She dropped her Coach bag down on the counter and sat in my salon chair.

"Hey, Leslie," Nora spoke.

"What's up?" Leslie spoke as she brushed her Brazilian hair out of her face.

I walked over to Nora and handed her the money. I noticed that Nora had a look on her face as she watched Leslie. It was a look of familiarity, like maybe she knew her or something. Something about the look was strange, or maybe I was just reading her wrong. I put the money in her hand and she bounced.

"So what are you plans when you first get there?" I turned to Leslie.

"You know, see my man, have lunch, do some shopping, then whip it on him before the night is over. Tomorrow will be strictly business. We are supposed to be meeting with a real estate agent at ten in the morning. He arranged for us to look at like six houses and if none of those work out, we are booked to look at several more the following day. After that, I will be back on a plane flying here to get packed and ready to start my new life."

"Hmmmph, I guess you have it all planned out." I grinned.

"I guess you can say that. Life is short. A plan is the best thing I need right now."

"That could be true."

I pulled her head back and started working my magic on her eyebrows. Before long they were on point and she was out. I thought about what she said about life being short and having a plan. These days, I didn't think much about plans like I had done in the past. I guess there was no time for thinking any more.

Chapter 22

After a long day at the salon, I was happy to get home and find out that Hood was already there. That was the perfect ending to my long, grumpy day. Stepping into the foyer, I heard the television up loud and I could tell by the actor's voice that he was watching *American Gangster*, one of his favorite movies. I rounded the corner and smiled at the sight of him. He looked so relaxed. I loved when we were home together.

"Hey, babe." He looked up at me. "Come on over here and sit next to me," he invited with a welcoming grin.

"I don't mind if I do."

I kicked off my shoes and strolled over. Bouncing down next to him, I leaned my head all the way back and our lips met. His lips were warm and inviting. I tingled all over. Only Hood could make me this way.

"Ummm," I moaned, savoring his taste.

Before he could control himself, his hands were under my shirt and cupping my breasts. In no time, my pants were on the floor and were quickly followed by my Victoria's Secret panties. I mounted him and went for the mountaintop. Panting and out of breath, we kissed each other deeply. Our lovemaking always left us speechless. Cradling me in his arms, we went back to watching the movie.

I don't know when I dozed off, but the ringing of Hood's cell phone was what stirred me. I was so sleepy that my body fought not to respond. But eventually my left eyelid opened halfway. Reluctantly, Hood grabbed his cell and looked at the caller ID. I lifted my head off of the pillow a bit so that I could look at him. I could see he was not happy about being disturbed.

"Damn! I told them niggas I was chillin' tonight!" He finally hit the answer button and barked into the speaker, "This betta be good!"

He was quiet and his eyes roamed the room as he listened to the caller on the other end. I noticed he became irritated and his breathing uneven. I knew this call was not good. I rose up.

Hood then sat up and put both his feet flat on the floor. "Tell her we can set it up in two days. That is when Lonzo will be back on point."

I could hear the person on the other end disagreeing.

"A'ight, fuck it. Set it up with her in two hours. But if she is one minute late, it's off. No questions asked." Hood was final and he ended the call.

The only thing on my mind was that "she" word he was using again. Who was she? Hanging up the phone, Hood started babbling that he had to step out. Something about Quad and one of his spots. To me it sounded like blah, blah, blah.

"Why can't Lonzo do it?" I didn't want him to leave. I wanted to sleep on the couch in his arms all night.

"Lonzo is out of town for a few days, and besides, Quad requested me," he informed me.

I did not like the sound of that. Who the fuck was she?

"Requested?" I spat. "What makes that bitch think she can request you? Hmmph, you need to check that 'cause Detroit ain't even her city."

Hood continued strapping up his Jordans, which had been residing next to the sofa. He looked up at me. "I know, but shit already stupid right now. I'ma handle it."

He was up on his feet and kissed me. And just like that, he was out.

Here I was again in this big house alone. Pouting, I dragged over and reset the alarm, then headed for the stairs. All I could do was shake my head thinking about that bitch Quad.

Before I could make it up the stairs, I heard banging on the door. Maybe Hood had left his keys. Turning around, I raced back down the stairs, turned off the alarm, unlocked the deadbolts, and I opened the door. I found myself face-to-face with my mother.

My heart dropped at the sight of her big, red eyes swollen from crying and two big roller suitcases next to her.

"Ma, what happened?"

Sniffing, she said, "I left your dad and I need to move in with you and Hood. I hate to intrude, but I cannot go back."

"Don't worry about that Ma, come on in."

I peeked outside into darkness as I reached down and grabbed the suitcases. I followed Ma into the kitchen, where she opened the refrigerator and retrieved a bottle of water. I stood back and observed. I wanted to give her a minute. Opening the water, she drank it halfway down.

"I ain't going back to him, Mya."

She sounded like she was trying to convince herself and not me. I just listened. I knew she had good reasoning, I just wanted to hear what it was.

"I think he is back in that life. His ass ain't never home, always the streets first. I did not come this far, fight this hard to get off drugs and turn my life around, all so he can get out of prison and mess it up. As much as I hate to say it, our marriage is not that important."

Then the tears once again took over. I figured it broke her heart to even say that last statement. At this point I did not know what to say; all I wanted to do was comfort her.

"Awww, Ma." I reached out and embraced her. She cried on my shoulder. I felt helpless, but I wanted to kick Dad in his black butt.

It took a minute but I finally got Ma calmed down enough to take a hot shower and go to bed. I was mentally exhausted. I climbed into my own bed but I could not find sleep. My mind rested on Hood and Quad. Picking up my cell phone, I looked at the time and realized Hood had already been gone for four hours. Scrolling through my phone, I pressed Hood. After three rings, I was sent straight to voicemail. For the first time ever, jealously swept over me. Now, I don't know where that feeling came from, but I did not like the way it felt. I tossed the phone to the right side of me and was out like a light.

Chapter 23

Rolling over, I felt Hood in bed next to me. I didn't know when or what time he came in, but I was not happy. He should have at least woke me up and said he was home. Especially when I had waited on him. He looked to be in deep, peaceful sleep. Snatching the cover completely off him, I rolled back over as if I was still asleep. I wanted him to feel annoyed, just as I felt. Not a minute later, I felt him easing his way back up under the covers next to me. I allowed him to get settled, then I snatched the cover off again. Even though I was salty with him, I almost laughed.

Groggily he protested, "Babe, why you won't share the blanket?"

He started to reach again but I moved over farther. I was enjoying this too much.

"I don't share with people who creep inside the house and into bed," I pouted.

"Come on, babe! I know you ain't trippin'. I got held up longer than I intended. When I made it home, you were resting so good and I decided not to wake you," he explained in his defense. But I was not letting him off that easy.

"So who were you held up with? Quad?" I made it more of statement than a question.

"Ah, no." He looked at me strangely, then he smiled. "I know you ain't jealous. Babe, you ain't never been jealous." He chuckled.

"What so funny?" I threw my pillow at him. "And I ain't jealous, but Quad better not get it twisted."

Grinning, Hood caught my pillow and rested his elbow on top of it. When he looked at me, I could tell he was sleepy as ever. "You don't have nothin' to worry about, I belong to you."

"I know." I bobbed my head down on the bed with a grin. Then it hit me. "Oh, Ma is here. She showed up last night right after you left. She is leaving Dad," I spilled.

Hood gave me a confused look. "Why?"

"She said that she thinks that he is back in the life." I shrugged my shoulders. "Oh, and he ain't never home no more."

"That's crazy."

I knew he did not want to say much because he did not want to take sides. I didn't either, but I knew Ma did not leave him for nothing. She was upset.

"I was thinking the same thing. But I put her

in the one of the guest rooms, so she will be here until whenever, I guess."

"That's cool. But what about your dad? He gone be over there all lonely."

"Wait, what? You mean like you gone be?"

I snatched my pillow from him and started playfully hitting him with it. We played around for a minute until we were both tired and sleepy again. My husband is my new best friend.

Chapter 24

"**D**ad, for the one thousandth time, I am not the one you should be talkin' to about this. Call Ma. What do you expect me to do?"

I was trying to put away a shipment that had come in, and to be honest, he was distracting me. Following me around, nagging at me about the situation with Ma. I mean, honestly, what did he expect me to do? Go home and tell her to pack her shit and move back into the condo with him? No, that was his business. He messed it up, now he could just figure out how to fix it.

"Baby Girl, you could talk to her and try to reason with her. Because right now she just don't hear nothing I have to say. It's like talking to a brick wall."

"Have you thought that maybe it's a reason for that?" I bent down to open another box. I was the last person to feel sorry for him right now. 'Cause I knew Ma was partially right.

"Okay, well, how can I explain myself if she won't answer my calls? Huh, how do I get around that? She has not answered one of my calls since she left."

"Dad, she is concerned about what you into. And why are you spending so much time in the streets? Answer that for me?" I decided to ask myself. If he couldn't give me a straight answer, how would he give her one?

"Look, she is exaggerating! I'm not out that much. I think she just don't want me to go anywhere. I mean, yeah, I hang out here and there with Big Nick. You know, go to the bar and grab a drink or somethin'. But's that's it. Plus she be working, so we just be missing each other sometime. That's all."

"Well, like I said, I'm not the one you have to convince. It's her." I hated being so nonchalant, but it was what it was.

I knew it was weighing on him. He was missing her. They had been through a lot together and the fact of the matter was that he loved her, he always had.

"Look, just give her some time and maybe she will come around."

His cell phone started to ring. He pulled it out fast and the look on his face told me that he was hoping that it was Mom. But even I knew that he was not that lucky. That woman could be stubborn. When his jaws dropped in disappointment, I knew it was not her.

"Hello?" He even sounded disappointed.

"Hello," he repeated. This time his face was weary, almost helpless. Without saying a word, he slowly hung up the phone. I got the feeling something was wrong.

"Dad, are you okay?"

He quickly changed his mood and smiled. "Yes, everything's cool. They had the wrong number."

I felt like he was not being truthful, but I shrugged it off.

"Ummm, look, I have to get going. Put in a good word with your momma for me if you can."

After all that I had said, he still wanted me to talk with Ma. I swear that man just did not listen.

━━━◉◉◉◉━━━

I decided to take off early from the salon. I had just been spending too much time there lately. So after putting away the order, I called Monica. I thought we could chat about Ma and Dad's situation. Maybe she had a conclusion. But after calling her several times unsuccessfully, I decided to go over. I called Ma up and told her to get dressed. I was going to swing by the house and pick her up. We were going to give Monica a surprise visit.

No questions asked, Ma was game. The drive took a minute but in no time we were pulling up to Palmar Woods, where Monica was now living in a mini mansion. The home was nice. It was baronial Tudor, nice and historic. It was clear that Rich had done well for himself. I just knew that a butler would answer when I rang the door-bell, but instead it was Monica, whose mouth flew open with excitement.

"What are you all doing here?" She threw her arms around Ma, who was standing in front of me.

"Well, we thought we would come make sure you were still alive since you can't answer your phone," I said sarcastically.

She reached around Ma and playfully nudged my shoulder. "Whatever, Mya, with your big-headed self. I lost my phone yesterday and I got to get out of here and go buy me a new one."

"It would be nice if you called and told someone that, especially with you living all the way out here in no man's land. Something important could have happened." I had to give her a hard time.

"Ain't you the one to talk, it's not like you live around the corner."

We loved to fuss at each other. Because we knew it was nothing but love.

"Oh, would both of you be quiet," Ma intervened with a grin.

"Oh, come on in."

She grabbed me by the arm and pulled me inside the huge house.

"And where is my grandbaby?" Ma asked right away.

"She's at her school care program. I have to pick her up in about two hours."

"Dang, I was looking forward to seeing her. I thought eventually you would stop taking her since you live out this far."

"No, Ma, she loves that place."

"I guess." Ma was disappointed. "I'm just going to have to come pick her up for the weekend."

"Well, you know you can have her whenever you want. Come on, let me take you guys on a tour."

The house was nice. The rooms were big and spacious with the original crown moldings and all. She said that Rich had spent hundreds of thousands of dollars having the home restored. It was beautiful. I thought the fireplace was to die for: it was marble and stretched up to the ceiling beams. Ma *oooh*ed and *ahhh*ed through the whole house.

Our last stop was the kitchen, where we all had a seat. Then Ma dropped the bombshell on Monica. She had been planning for a week as to how she would break the news to her and I had been sworn to secrecy.

"I left your dad and moved in with Mya."

"What!" Monica yelled.

"I moved out," she repeated. "I had to—things are just not working out."

"Why? Ma, what has he done?"

"For starters he ain't never home. Then, there is them damn streets, he just can't let go. I don't know exactly what he is into, but I'm not having a good feeling about any of it. So I just removed myself from the situation."

Monica looked at her then me. When she saw that I had nothing to say, her gaze went back to Ma.

"What does Dad have to say?"

"I don't know. I haven't talked to him. I'm not ready."

"Well, don't you want to at least give him a chance to explain, Momma?" Monica sounded like a little girl.

"Look . . ." The look on Ma's face was stern. "Now I won't sit here and debate this matter. I did what I thought was best. Just as you thought moving in with this Rich was better for you. When I am ready to talk with your father, I will. Okay?"

Monica seemed surprised that Ma had gone there. "Okay, I'm sorry. I didn't mean anything by it. It's just that you two have been together for so long and through so much."

A tear escaped Monica's left eye, but she quickly wiped it away.

"It's all right." Ma smiled. "It will be all right."

"Now that's over with, what snacks do you have out here? I need something."

I got up and went straight for the huge fridge.

Chapter 25

It had been a couple of weeks since I had dropped by to see Mrs. Wynita and Tiny, so I went by and visited with them. They were glad to see me. Mrs. Wynita was still holding out hope that Rochelle would return. According to her, Rochelle had not been by to see Tiny in weeks. But she had called a few times just to see if they were okay. She said Rochelle still sounded strange over the phone. Nevertheless, she was glad for the calls, because they helped keep Tiny satisfied, and she wanted to keep Tiny's life as normal as possible.

I told her of my attempts to catch up with Rochelle even after all that bull she pulled on me at the club. I still went by periodically trying to catch her at home, but I never could catch her there, or she was hiding; either way, I had no success. After I left Mrs. Wynita's, I went to the salon to check on things. I didn't have any appointments scheduled so I didn't plan to stay long. When I pulled up and made my way inside, everything looked cool. The only thing I felt was missing was the sound of Rochelle playing around talking shit. I could still hear her silly laughter in my mind. If she didn't have a client, she would be up front in Pam's area jacking around. Then I would always try to play at being serious, telling her to be professional at work.

The only thing that made me do a double take once I was inside of the salon was the sight of Kalil standing at the receptionist area. I quickly wondered if Rochelle was in the back choking Nora.

Boldly he turned to me. "Just the lady I have been looking for."

Pam's eyes looked as if they wanted to explain. She knew that I did not welcome him here.

"And why would you be lookin' for me?" I gave him attitude. "Is something wrong with Rochelle?" That was the only logical reason that I could think of that would cause him to look for me. Anything else would be void.

"Nah, she cool." He smirked and rubbed his nappy goatee. I could have slapped that silly look off his face.

"Then, what?" I asked impatiently. "Why are you here?"

"Well, this is a hair salon, isn't it?" He glanced around. Ugh! He made me sick.

"Look, get to the point or get out." I pointed toward the door. I hoped I was blunt enough.

"A'ight. Well, I was wondering if you could fade me up? Rochelle said that this was the best place in town and that you were the best one to do it."

For a second I wondered if I was being punked.

"Hah." I gave a sarcastic chuckle. I knew he was kidding. "Well, did she also tell you we don't take strays or walk-ins?" I decided to hit below the belt.

"You know what? It's cool, I was just trying to make your girl happy. I'll let her know you were real welcomin'."

That got my attention. The last thing I wanted was for him to go back and tell Rochelle that I was rude. I cared too much about what she would think, so I gave in.

"Kalil." I called his name just as he was about to walk out the door. He did not hesitate to stop, almost like he knew I would change my mind.

"Look, I can't do it, but I have someone else that can."

I refused to touch him and I didn't give a damn how Rochelle felt about that. I called Nora and asked her to prep to fade him up.

"So how is Rochelle?" I didn't want to talk to him but he would know.

"She straight," he answered shortly.

"Hmmph, well, she can't be doing that good if it's keeping her away from her daughter."

He looked at me and sucked his teeth but never responded.

"You should try telling her to go home to her daughter."

"I'm Rochelle's man, not her daddy, a'ight. I don't tell her what to do."

He smirked and it took everything in me not spit in his face. Instead, I rolled my eyes at him and walked away. He could kiss my ass.

I passed Nora just as she came out to retrieve him. I almost told her to forget it, but I had Rochelle on my conscience.

"Fucking ugly bastard," I mumbled to no one in particular. Maybe Nora's clippers would slip and then go zigzag on his head.

Chapter 26

It was Rich's birthday and he was having a huge bash at the club. Everyone except Hood was there. I hated it but I promised to turn up for him. Monica had a smile on her face that couldn't be wiped off. She was happy to celebrate for her man and Rich relished it. He loved the attention. He had spared no cost for his birthday. He even had Rick Ross come out to perform at his party. The club was jam-packed, wall to wall.

Even though we had waited to the last minute to pull together our outfits, Monica I were dressed to kill. Monica was rocking a L'Agence tuxedo jumpsuit with a pair of Christian Louboutin Iriza crystal pumps. I complemented her in my strapless Milly jumpsuit that was topped off with a pair of Yves Saint Laurent studded leather pumps. We were some bad bitches and the compliments were rolling in.

We had just finished getting our groove on to Rick Ross and T-Pain's "Bag of Money" when it was time to sing "Happy Birthday" to Rich. Monica had had a cake made with an oversize picture of him sitting on a Maybach on it. The grin on his face showed that he loved it.

Just as Rich cut into his cake, I looked down and saw Quad and her crew making their way into the club, looking like they owned the place. She had been pointed out to me by a friend before so I recognized her instantly. As if it was not enough, the DJ gave them a big shout-out. My eyes followed them all the way to their VIP room.

"Damn, it's like that. They shoutin' that bitch out." Leslie looked at me like I had the answer, as she looked below and watched them swag to their VIP area. "Rich must know her."

"I don't know." I shrugged then took a shot of Hennessy, then another.

Leslie, Monica, Trina, and I and hit the dance floor and we stayed on it all night as the good times rolled. As we danced, I noticed C-Lo, one of Hood's workers, kept trying to get Monica to dance with him. Clearly, he did not know that Monica was with Rich, or he just didn't give a fuck, because he would not let up.

Rich had been in and out of the room pretty much all night. Even though it was his birthday party, it was his club and he wanted to watch his money, so he kept getting up. Eventually, he saw

C-Lo in Monica's ear. He walked up to Monica and snatched her by the wrist. My eyes zoomed in on this just as I decided to sit down.

I jumped out of my seat and got up in Rich's face. "Yo, motherfucker, why you snatchin' on her!"

"I ain't snatch her." He tried to sound calm. But I knew he was pissed. It was written all over his face.

"Nigga, I ain't blind. I just saw you snatch her arm." I turned to Monica. "You just gone let him snatch you like that? He don't look shit like Lester to me," I said, referring to our dad.

Monica's eyes pleaded with me because she knew it was about to go down. "Mya, it ain't like that. Don't trip."

I ignored her and turned my attention back to Rich. I grabbed a Patrón bottle that was close to me. I was ready to bust his head wide open. Trina grabbed me back.

"You betta check yourself because shit just got real. Don't you ever snatch on her!" I threw the bottle as I broke free of Trina. Lucky for Rich, he was quick on his feet. He ducked and I missed his head by about an inch.

"Mya, calm down! It was not like that!" Monica pulled me away from Rich and wrapped her arms around me. "Mya, just chill."

I took a deep breath, my eyes still glued to Rich, who was still bent down in his duck stance. I looked at Monica. "You betta check that nigga, Monica, 'cause his future won't look too bright if this shit happens again."

"I know, he just in his feelings right now

about C-Lo tryin' to push up on me. That's all."
She continued to try to explain but that went
over my head. I could care less about his reasons.

"You know what, Monica? I don't give a
fuck, as long as you heard what I said! I'm out."
I snatched away from her and walked away.

Just as I stepped out of VIP and started making my way down the steps, I noticed Quad
watching me and we locked eyes. Quad and her
goons stepped out of their VIP area followed by
two females. We walked past each other and
bumped shoulders. Already upset, I got offended.

"You got a problem?" I sneered at Quad without warning.

Quad started laughing like I was funny. "Bitch,
do you know who I am?" she had the nerve to ask.

"No, the question is, do you know me, bitch!"
I spat.

Quad just stared at me as if she wanted to
figure me out, then she lifted the shot glass in
her hand and polished off her drink. I knew
then that the bitch was trying to annoy me and I
did not have the time.

"Just stay out of my way next time, bitch." I
was done with her so I threw my hand up to dismiss her. That must have struck a chord because
her whole demeanor changed.

"Bitch, that's enough disrespect. My whole
crew in this motherfucker—" She paused. "But I
happen to know you Hood's li'l wifey, so I'ma
give you a pass. 'Cause normally, I dead disrespect."

Then her bodyguard stepped up. Now that I took as a threat. I went wild screaming as the bouncers tried to hold me back. "Is that a threat, bitch? Then let's Glock! Right outside, hoe!" Before I knew it, I had been pulled outside the club.

"Mya, calm down," Trina and Leslie kept chanting repeatedly.

"Fuck her anyway, she just talking shit," Leslie yelled.

"Fuck this, I'm out." I popped the locks on my Range Rover and balled out. As soon as I opened the front door of my house, I yelled out for Hood.

"Babe, I'm in the kitchen."

I threw my key down on the counter; I was heated. "What's up with that bitch Quad?"

Hood looked at me, confused. Before he could say a word, I went in. "That bitch tried it tonight. Are you fuckin' her or something?"

Hood's eyes got big like circles.

"Yo, what the fuck is going on?"

"Nigga, you betta answer me!"

"Hell, no! Now tell me what happened."

"I don't know. I was leaving the club and I caught the bitch staring at me. The next thing I know, we bumped shoulders and one word led to another so we was going in. Then, the bitch gone threaten me. And you know I don't take too kindly to that."

"Man, I don't know what's up with that shit. But I'ma check that bitch."

"You betta or I will 'cause she got me fucked up."

Hood's eyes followed me as I reached for a peanut butter cookie on the table where he had been eating. I had to eat something sweet to help me calm down.

"I can't believe you thought I was smashing her. That bitch is a dyke."

"Hmmmph." I almost choked on my cookie.

"She like girls, babe." Hood started laughing.

"Well, somebody betta tell her, I ain't her bitch. Always some bullshit."

I grabbed another cookie and stormed off toward the stairs. I was going to bed. Hood followed, taunting me.

Chapter 27

Things were cool over the next couple of weeks. There was no real face-to-face drama with anyone and I welcomed that with opened arms. I was beyond sick of the bullshit. Ma had still not gotten back with Dad. That kind of saddened me, but at the same time I respected her decision. So while I had her at home with me I made good use of it. We stayed up late nights, watching movies and talking about our past lives in the Brewster. While a lot of them were bad memories, there turned out to be a lot of good ones. So we laughed into late hours of the night.

I was still hanging out in the cold on the Rochelle situation. She was still MIA. While my heart ached every day over it, I prayed and kept it moving. I had to believe that she would snap out of it. I just felt like if my mother could bounce back from a full crack addiction, then anyone had the ability to change. Because one thing I knew for sure, she loved Tiny and eventually she would turn her life around for her.

"What are you doing here, Ma?" I sucked the bone of one of the hot wings that I had been gnawing on for lunch. I was sitting in my booth area taking a quick lunch when she strolled in.

"I came by to meet up with your dad."

That was shocking: the last I knew they were not even talking. "Oh," was my only reply. She knew that I was wondering what was going on.

"Why you say it like that?"

"Like what?" I smiled.

"You know how you said it."

"No, for real, Ma. I was just saying oh. I mean it's been a minute and you never even hinted that you even talked to him."

"Well, it's not like that. He called and said he wanted to show me something and I figured, why not." She shrugged it off like it was no big deal.

"Hey, you don't have to explain to me. That is your husband." I continued to smile as I put a fry in my mouth. "But since we on the subject, how are things with you two?" I figured that I might as well ask. Now would be a better time than any.

She looked at me and playfully rolled her eyes while she considered my question. She reached into my plate and grabbed a few fries. She chewed on them slowly, then sucked her teeth.

"I guess you can say cool. We have talked a

few times over the past couple of days. He has been trying to prove to me that he is a changed man."

"That is good, Ma."

I was happy to hear her say that. I wanted nothing more than for them to get back together. But I also wanted nothing than more for her than to be happy. And if that meant not being with Dad, then I would have to agree.

"I told him that words are okay, but I need to see it first. I'm from the old school and I know all too well that action speaks louder than words ever can. So he just better be prepared to do that. 'Cause I ain't puttin' up with no mess."

"What mess you ain't puttin' up with?" Monica strolled in, all teeth and gums.

Ma and I both looked at her and wondered why she was so happy. She was in the salon every two weeks to get her hair done. And she hardly ever came in grinning, so something was up.

"I was talkin' about me and your dad. Why you grinning like a Cheshire cat?"

"Who, me? Just smiling on this beautiful day. That's all. So what about you and Dad? Are you two back together?"

"No, but we have been communicating a little. That is why I'm here. He asked me to meet him."

"Now that's what's up." Monica was not shy about showing her enthusiasm for them getting back together. But we knew that would be her response.

"Calm down. Nothing is official yet," Ma warned just as Dad walked in.

"I know, I know. Anywho, look at what Rich got me." She held out a key, one that I recognized as being a Mercedes key.

"Hmmph, so is that his 'I'm sorry' gift?" I was not impressed. Hell, I could buy her a Mercedes. As far as I was concerned, she didn't need anything from him.

Ma just looked at the both of us. "Well, is it, Monica?" she asked when it took Monica too long to answer me.

"Nooo . . . he got me that so I can have more than one whip. That's all. Rich likes his woman having the best."

"Well, I hope understands that you don't need him to buy you anything. All you have to do is come to me."

"Mya, I know and so does Rich. But he is my man now and if he wants to blow money on me, then why not? Come on, he is a good guy. Just give him a chance, Mya," she pleaded with a smile.

"Whatever you say . . . and why have you not been coming around?"

"I have been busy with school and getting Imani back and forth. By the time I get in at night, I'm bushed."

I wanted to believe her, but I was not sure if I should. She liked Rich and was willing to say anything to get us to like him too. So I decided not to soften so easy.

"All right, that's what you say, but that nigga betta not be tryin' to control nothin'."

"I swear it is not like that."

"It betta not be, 'cause your dad will kill

him," Ma threatened as she stared a hole into Monica. "And that's if I don't get to him first." That was a promise.

Monica chuckled just as Dad entered. He spoke to us but made it clear that we were not his number one priority. He walked over to Ma, softly kissed her on the cheek, then asked her if she was ready.

Ma did not smile but I could see her heart soften at the sight of him. In a soft tone she told him that she was ready. They both quickly told us good-bye and left.

We smiled as we watched them leave. "Dang, I hope they get back together," Monica said.

"I know, right."

"So you got time to hook me up?" Monica rubbed her hand through her hair.

"Uhhh, you do need an appointment, ma'am," I said playfully.

"Oh, so it's like that now? All right." Monica acted like she was about to leave.

"Bring your spoiled butt and sit in this chair." I closed the lid on my hot wings and stood up.

Chapter 28

"Mya, I just don't know. I might go, though I just keep second-guessing. Especially since that last date I tried. That shit was a mess, but I guess you can't compare the two," Trina vented.

She had been conversing with this guy that she had been introduced to and they had been on a few dates, which all turned out good. Now he wanted to take her to Vegas for a weekend. Of course, she came to me hoping that I could give her advice on what to do. For some reason, people always thought I knew what to do. But I almost felt clueless about everything myself. Who was to say what was the right or the wrong decision. Normally, I would take my questions to Rochelle looking for advice.

"Look, you have to make this decision on your own. Weigh all of your pros and cons. To be honest, since you have been dating him, everything has been going good. Dude seems like a really good guy. Plus he's close to your family. That is why you agreed to go out on the first date with him. That has to count for something."

"Yeah, I guess you are right." She seemed to be considering what I had said. But I could sense that something was still bugging her. She sighed, then looked away. "Something I hate to admit is that it has a lot to do with Teddy."

That was a name I had not heard her use in a long time. Hearing her bring up his name sort of upset me. That dude was a loser, always beating on Trina and making her feel low just because he was a creep, but in the end, he had gotten what he deserved. Trina didn't need to waste one moment thinking about him. He was not worth the spit it would take to wet him.

"Sometimes I think about him and I shake—remembering all the things he did to me. It just makes me afraid to date or get serious with someone. What if I meet another him?"

"Fuck Teddy with his punk ass."

Trina looked at me with shock on her face. I don't think she saw that coming. But I had to be real and that was exactly how I felt.

"Trina, you cannot let him end your life. If you were going to do that, you may as well have stayed with him. You are not the scared woman that he was used to. You are strong and you have taken control of your life."

A tear slid down Trina's left cheek. She wiped it away and shook her head in agreement with what I was saying.

"You keep living, and whether or not you are ready to take that step and go to Vegas, let it be your choice, from your own heart."

More tears had fallen, but Trina had managed to dry them all. Her voice was still shaky when she said, "You are right, Mya. Thank you, girl."

"You know I got you." I grinned.

Out of nowhere, in strolled Leslie. Secretly, I laughed and wondered if I should offer her a job. After all, she spent all her spare time at the salon. At first she always told me when she was stopping by. But now she just popped up. I mean we were cool and all, but I was running a business, not a meeting place.

"What's up, chic?" I spoke and Trina did, too.

"Girl, I had to stop by to let you know that I found out where your boy Kalil lives."

Now that was information I wanted to know, so I became all ears and Leslie was sure not to disappoint. She gave me the run-down all the way to Kalil's front door with her directions. I was not going to get lost. I was also learning that Leslie was a little resourceful. I would miss her when she moved away. She was supposed to be gone by now, but some things had come up that she had to take care of. Although the crib had been picked and paid for, according to her, her move was put off a bit.

"Thanks, Leslie. Good lookin' out."

I was distressed but at least I knew how to find Rochelle now.

"It was nothing," she commented as Nora stepped into the room.

"I will be making my way over there soon."

"Well, I wish you well. But listen, I got to go, trying to get this shit wrapped up so I can make this move."

"A'ight."

Pam walked in the room and told Trina that someone wanted to speak with her, so she left the room also. Nora was still standing in the room looking like she had something on her mind.

"Mya, remember I told you I thought your girl Leslie looked familiar to me? Now I remember where I saw her. She was at one of my cousin's parties. You know I told you about my cousin that was deep in the drug life, the one that just got out like a year ago."

"Yeah, I remember."

"Well, your homegirl Leslie dates one of his friends and I have seen her at one of those parties. Matter of fact, I think I've seen her at more than one. I can't really remember dude's name, though. He a cutie, too—" Nora paused. I could tell she was racking her brain to remember what the guy's name is.

As I turned off my equipment, I kinda of thought about what she was saying. It must have been an old guy Leslie had dated or something. Either way, my mind quickly reverted back to Rochelle. I had to go visit her at Kalil's.

"Alonzo," Nora said, breaking into my thoughts. I look at her, clueless. "I think that is the dude's name." Nora smiled, happy that she had remembered.

"Okay," I answered.

I was eager to get back to what I was planning. I had to convince Rochelle to come home. But how would I? What could I say to convince her? She would probably tell me to get out. And hell, that is even if she allowed me to come in. But none of that mattered, I had to at least try. There was no way I could just give up on her. Not yet.

Chapter 29

I decided that I could not waste any time so instead of going home after leaving the salon, I headed straight to Kalil's house. As I pulled into his driveway, I saw Rochelle's Mercedes truck parked outside. That meant that she was there, unless she was gone somewhere with Kalil. I doubted that, because there was a newly revamped Chevy Caprice with the butterfly doors on it and an Audi sport parked outside. I figured one or both had to belong to him. He was so damned ghetto, I would bet money that the Chevy Caprice definitely belonged to him.

Stepping out of my vehicle, I hit the lock before taking a look around the neighborhood. It was not too bad; not necessarily the ghetto, it was in a middle class section of Detroit. I had my Ruger tucked in my side just in case something popped off and I had to bust a cap in Kalil's punk ass. All he had to do was give me a reason. But on the other hand, shooting him was the last thing I needed to do. Rochelle would cast me out as the devil. So I would try to chill.

I knocked on the door and after three knocks, there was no answer. I sighed and turned to leave, because if I knocked one more time, I would use my gun and shoot the knob off, because I knew someone was inside. Before I could walk away, the door opened. I turned and came face to face with Kalil. The look in his eyes told me everything I needed to know. He was high.

It was just too hard to try and hide my attitude, so I just went with it. "Where Rochelle at?"

"Damn, no hi or nothin'." He grinned. In the background I heard Rochelle yell, "What's that?"

"Nothin'," he answered, still grinning.

With a gesture of his hand, he invited me in, then slammed the door. I stood in the short hallway looking around. The house smelled like fried chicken and air freshener. The walls were painted pale beige with dark brown trim. Whoever painted had no imagination. Kalil stepped around me and started walking, so I followed. The first door we passed on the left was open. I glanced in and noticed that it was a bathroom. Then we approached the second doorway off the right and walked through it. I continued following him and we landed in the living room. Rochelle was there lying on a powder blue and white sofa watching *The Facts of Life*.

Without turning around, she asked, "Who was at the door, Kalil? I heard you slam it."

I decided to speak before him. "Hey, Rochelle."

Just like Linda Blair, Rochelle sat up and snapped her head around at me. I thought she had broken her neck with all that force. Clearly, she was shocked, but the look on her face was calm.

"Oh my God!" She started laughing. The laugh threw me off. It was sort of wicked. "How did you find me?" She started to shake her head. "Damn, I cannot get away from you." Then the calmness disappeared. She was upset and did not want me there. But this much I had assumed, so I was not surprised.

She turned to Kalil, who was standing behind me. "Why did you let her in here?"

"Shit, I don't know. She came to see you." His attitude was nonchalant.

She rolled her eyes at him and, without looking at me, Rochelle turned back around toward the television. I had come for a reason, so I would not just let her dismiss me and walk away. Slowly, I started walking toward her.

"Rochelle . . ." My voice was soft and steady. "Look, I did not come over here to fight or argue with you. I—" I cleared my throat. "I just wanted to check on you. I wanted to be sure you were all right."

She turned back to face me. "Why, Mya? Why do you feel the need to check on me?"

"Because I have been worried about you."

"Well, you have seen me. Now you can leave."

I stood glued to my spot. Her smart mouth was annoying, but I did my best to ignore that part.

"What about Tiny? When do you think you going home to her? She misses you. Or have you cut her off, too?"

Tiny was her soft spot. She cast her eyes downward.

"Maybe you should just go like she said," Kalil spoke up and stood next to me.

The mere sound of his voice pissed me off. I looked over at him and anger overtook me. "Fuck you, Kalil, and don't say shit else to me. Look at what you are doing to my friend. You ain't shit but a pill poppin' fiend."

Again, he started laughing at me, but I knew it was nothing but the drugs. Out of nowhere Rochelle jumped up off the couch.

"Don't you come up in my man's house disrespecting him. You got some fucking nerve, Mya. Oh, wait, now I see . . . that is what you want from me. Ain't takin' two of my men . . ." She held up two fingers in my face. "Ain't two enough? Yeah, two," she repeated. "Li'l Lo and Todd were both killed because of your bullshit. All of it was because of you, my supposed-to-be best friend. I guess you just ain't gone be happy until you steal all my joy. Todd was my last shot at happiness. An innocent, good man shot up because you were not honest with me. So please just leave me in peace. Just get out, Mya!"

My face was covered in tears and so was my heart. She had finally said it all without beating around the bush. Whatever became of her would be on me. I had single-handedly caused her a world of unhappiness. How could I give it back was the question. The answer was I couldn't.

"If that is what you want, Rochelle, then you got it."

Walking out of that house, away from my childhood best friend, was one of the hardest things that I have ever had to do. But it had to be done. I owed her that much.

Chapter 30

I was in bed for a few days after I visited Rochelle. I was physically sick from the incident and the realization that it was what it was. I decided not to tell Hood about it. I wasn't keeping it a secret, I just didn't feel like talking about it. I wanted to forget it ever happened and move on. But the moment he saw me lying around, he started nagging me to find out what was wrong. I told him that I couldn't get out of bed because I was having bad cramps, because that was the only way I was going to get him out of the house otherwise. Anytime he thought something was bothering me emotionally or physically, he wanted to be there for me.

Today I decided what I needed was fresh air. I would go outside, sit on my patio by the pool, and soak up the sun. I had to drag myself out of my bed, but once inside the hot shower I started to come alive. I threw on a pair of baby pink tennis shorts and a white wifebeater and I was ready to head outside. But first I would grab me a slush. I had to gear my slush machine up, though—it had been a while since I used it. I grabbed J. California Cooper's novel *Life is Short But Wide* off the nightstand when I heard Hood come in the house yelling my name.

With my book in hand, I raced down the stairs. The sound of his voice told me it was urgent. I found him at the edge of the stairway. His eyes found mine.

"Babe, what's wrong?"

"My trap houses missin' about two million in cash. Shit is just gone." In the business Hood was in, two million dollars was not exactly a lot of money. But when you are talking about cold, hard cash it was. This was a problem. I was so damned shocked I was nervous.

"What the hell happened?" I managed.

"I don't know. But I'm about to find out. These li'l fucking chucks acting innocent and dumb. But they know betta. This shit gone get some answers and I mean tonight. I just wanted to let you know shit about to be crazy. I came home to suit up with some extra shit." His cell phone started to ring. He answered it right away and immediately started yelling nigga this or that.

Then my house phone started to ring, which was out of the ordinary. The only person who ever called it was Ma when she could not reach me on my cell. She knew I was home, so it had to be her. As soon as I answered she confirmed it. "Mya." She was talking fast.

"Hey, Ma."

"Look, you need to go over to Monica's house and check on her. She was on my mind this morning, so I called her up to speak with her for a bit. I don't know, she just sounded strange on the phone to me. She was like short with her answers. I don't know. She was not typical Monica to me. It could be nothin', but I just want you to ride out and check on her."

"A'ight. I will go out there."

"Call me once you talk to her."

"I will." I ended the call just as Hood hung up his phone. "So is everything cool?"

"Nah, but I know what has to be done. I'ma get what I need, then I'ma be out."

This was always the hard part, but the last thing he needed was me freaking out. I had to be strong, or at least pretend like I was, when really I just wanted to scream, *Fuck that money, we have plenty, stay home.* But I knew I could not do that. He had to handle business.

"Call me later then," I said instead.

"Oh, who was that on the phone?" he asked, referring to my call.

"That was Ma. She wants me to check on Monica so I'ma head out that way."

Just like that, my plans to lie by the pool, drink my slush, and soak up the sun were a bust. I went back up to my room, threw on some clothes, and packed my worries about my husband inside my heart. I jumped in my truck and pointed it in the direction of the interstate that would lead straight to Monica's house.

Chapter 31

On my way to Monica's, I decided to make a quick stop by Starbucks. I needed something to give me energy. I was still in shock from Hood's revelation. I could not believe that some dummy thought that they could get away with stealing from him. There was only one place they would end up and that was in the morgue, and not because of the money. Hell, Hood had plenty of that. It was the principle. I shook my head at the thought as I exited the Starbucks parking lot. Just as I veered back on the interstate, Trina's name lit up on my cell phone. She was back from Vegas so I knew she wanted to fill me in on the trip. I was really happy when she told me she put all her fears aside and went.

"Hello."

"Hey, girl." I could hear the excitement in

her voice. That alone told me that she had a good time.

"So tell me. How was it?"

"Girl, Mya, I had so much fun. He was the perfect gentleman the whole time. He even got me my own room. We gambled, toured the sights, and just enjoyed ourselves. I almost didn't want to come back."

"See, I told you. Sometimes you just have to try new things."

"I know. I see it now. I'm so glad I went. But I just wanted to call you and thank you for the words of encouragement. I needed that. You are such a good friend, Mya."

"Awww, thanks. Now you tryna make me cry," I cooed.

"You better not." Trina laughed. "Anyway, I made it back late last night so I need to unpack. I will see you at the salon."

"Cool, talk to you then." I ended the call just as I was pulling into Monica's driveway. I took one last big gulp of my mocha cappuccino and jumped out of the car.

I walked to the front door and hit the doorbell. It opened so fast that I thought someone had to be standing behind it. It was Monica with what I knew to be a counterfeit smile plastered on her face. She spoke to me and turned quickly, heading deeper into the foyer area before I could respond. I turned and grabbed the doorknob and shut the huge-ass door.

"What's up?" I asked as I followed her.

"Nothin'. I was about to lie down. I'm not feeling well." The fact that she answered the door so quickly made me think that she was not being truthful. But I decided to wing it.

"Well, Ma thought you sounded kind of strange when she spoke with you earlier so she asked me to come over and check on you."

I could not see her face because she still had her back to me. But her tone almost sounded annoyed.

Monica sighed. "I'm cool."

Abruptly, she turned in my direction. My eyes went straight to the flushed looking area on the right side of her face. I looked at the left side of her face to compare the two before jumping to conclusions. My assumption was the right side of her face was either flushed or swollen.

"What the fuck happed to your face!"

Monica looked at me as though I was crazy and tried to play dumb. "Ain't nothin' wrong with my face."

"Don't bullshit me, Monica—" Then it hit me. "Oh, my God! Did Rich hit you?"

"Hell, no." She acted as if my question was absurd. "I had an allergic reaction to some shrimp the other night." She chuckled and rubbed the swollen area. "I didn't even know it still looked like that."

For a minute I considered what she had just said. I remembered this time in high school when one of my classmates had an allergic reaction to some ketchup. She had swollen like a melon. But something told me that Monica was lying. In fact, I knew it. Her actions told me that Rich was guilty.

I started shaking my head at her for being so

pathetic. "Why are you lying for him? Who the fuck do he think he is?" I was so upset my entire face was on fire.

Monica was still not ready to admit it to me. I was enraged and she was looking at me like I was overreacting. She sighed, throwing her hand up in a dramatic waving motion. "Mya, Rich did not hit me. He would not do that."

I was sick of her protecting him. Before I knew it I was in her face. "You have Imani to think about, and you slippin'. You been missing school and shit. I told you that moving in with him was a bad idea. You hardly even know this nigga. Did you ever think about that? I mean did you really ever take the time to think?"

I rubbed both of my temples, which were throbbing from pure aggravation. I knew she had no answer for me because she still didn't get it.

"Mya, stop actin' like you my fuckin' momma, okay!" she had the nerve to scream. "I got this. I love Rich and he loves Imani and me. Besides, I can finish school next year. Rich takes good care of us. I have to be there for him."

"So now you wanna depend on a nigga. Hmmph, didn't Ma teach you anything? She depended on Dad and we all saw what that got her." I hated that statement as soon as it left my mouth, but I was upset.

"Now you talkin' crazy and this shit is not the same."

I was breathing hard. I had to calm down. I was saying too much too fast. I needed to think rationally. This was hard for me.

"Look, I know I can be harsh and judgmental, but Rich can't be putting his hands on you . . . I won't have it and I think you know me well enough to know that. Now you need to pack your things and get Imani's things and let's go."

Monica looked at me and walked away. "I ain't going nowhere, so you can forget it. I am fine and Imani is fine. And just like always, you are overreacting for nothin'."

I guess she called being punched or slapped in the face nothin'.

"Nothin'," I repeated. "Monica, he hit you, and of all places in your face." I wanted to get through to her, but it was like hitting a brick wall.

Again she stopped walking just as we reached the kitchen entrance. She turned to me and yelled. "No, he did not, for the thousandth time!"

"Monica, I do not believe you," I said calmly. I was done yelling and being dramatic. "But you know I will fuck Rich up. I will body-bag his ass and watch him be toe-tagged. So you need to do the smart thing and get out of this relationship." She had been warned. I turned to leave, but suddenly I had something else to say. "And another thing: I don't like how he answers your cell phone all the time claimin' you busy. They call that shit being controlling."

"Well, Rich is not like that."

"Whatever, I gotta go."

I had to get out of there before I choked my own sister. I was pissed. It was time I had a chat with Rich.

Chapter 32

I burned rubber out of Monica's driveway and headed straight to Rich. I knew exactly where to find him: the Ripple Turn, his club. I went inside and spoke to some familiar faces. All the employees there knew me well. I had been going to this club way before Rich bought it.

Making my way to the back of the club, I barged into Rich's office where I found him on the phone. The look on his face showed me that he was surprised to see me. He held up a finger, as if telling me to give him a second. But I refused to acknowledge it. He was going to talk to me now.

"Hang up the phone now!" I demanded.

He covered up the phone so that the person on the other end of the line would not hear me and said, "Just a minute. This is important."

Clearly, he did not get the memo that I didn't give a fuck. I walked over the wall jack, snatched the phone cord out of the wall, and tossed it in his direction. Rich's mouth opened wide with surprise.

"I saw my sister today. And she ain't your punching bag. Keep your fucking hands off her before you find yourself in the morgue."

"Calm down, li'l momma. Can't we talk about this? Because I don't hit females, so you got the wrong information."

He was too calm for my taste. His ass was guilty as charged and he knew it.

"Rich, be a man. Don't lie. I don't know exactly what happened, but please believe me, I will pop a cap in your ass and sleep well that night. Now fuck you and good-bye."

———— ◈ ————

I figured that I would stop by the salon because it had been more than a week since I had been there. The parking lot was packed! Business was good as always. Just as I pulled into my parking space, Hood's name lit up on my phone. I prayed everything was cool.

"Hey, babe," I answered.

"Aye, I need you to meet me at the lockdown spot. Remember where it's at?"

"Yeah, I remember."

"A'ight, ASAP then."

Before I could ask him any more questions he hung up. My heart dropped. Something was wrong. The lockdown was an abandoned warehouse outside of town. I had only been there twice with Hood to pick something up. Never had he called me and told me to drive out there. Driving as fast as traffic would allow, I headed out. Once I made it outside of town, cars were scarce, which I gladly invited.

As I approached the entrance door, Hood opened it. I recognized the same distress on his face that was there earlier that day after finding out about the missing money.

"What's going on, babe?" I asked as soon as I was inside. The place smelled like roasted peanuts, but I ignored it.

"I found out who was responsible for the missing money . . ." He paused. "Lonzo."

"Lonzo? Ain't he like your new right-hand man?" I couldn't hide my shock.

"Yep, that nigga been foul."

Damn, that was messed up. But now I wondered why I was here.

"I called you here because of his accomplice."

Hood opened the door to a room to the left and told me to go in first. I stopped in my tracks and my heart sped up. I looked at Hood briefly, then turned back and came face to face with Leslie. She was tied to what looked like several mop and broom handles that were somehow attached to the wall. I grabbed my chest and took one step forward, but stopped and I turned to Hood.

"What is going on here? Why is Leslie tied up?"

"Why don't you ask your slick-ass friend?"

Before I could completely turn around to

face Leslie, I heard her scream, "I don't have to say shit to her!"

Hearing her say those words shocked me. But suddenly it all made sense. Nora had told me that Leslie was dating some guy named Alonzo. It clicked in my mind that it could be Lonzo.

"Wait, wait, so this is the dude you went to Chicago with? So you have been lying to me?"

I shook my head in disappointment. The whole time Leslie had the nerve to be giving me the side-eye.

"So what, bitch? Are you going to cry now? Bitch, cry over bloodshed." Leslie popped off again.

I did not know who the hell this chick was. I had never seen Leslie behave this way. I turned to Hood; maybe he had some answers. But Hood was shaking his head as well. He was just as shocked as I was.

"Baby, I can't believe it, either."

Her heartless statements were hurtful. We were supposed to be friends; instead this bitch was acting as if she was possessed. What was going on? Why would Leslie want to conspire with Lonzo to rob Hood? Why befriend me?

"I don't understand, Leslie. Why? Why are you doing this?" At this point nothing she said would really matter. I just wanted answers for confirmation.

"Is that what you want me to answer for you?"

"Aye, shut the fuck up! You don't have to say shit," Lonzo barked.

I looked in the direction that his angry voice came from. I hadn't even noticed that he was in the room when I entered. He was tied to an abandoned refrigerator. He had so much rope and cord tied to his shirtless, bruised body that it was sitting deep in his wounded flesh. When he spoke up, there was nothing but pain in his voice and facial expressions, but he still had the nerve to try to talk shit.

"Nigga, don't tell me to shut up," Leslie shouted at Lonzo, and spit flew out of her mouth. I could tell that he wanted to respond to her but his pain was unbearable.

"Right, nigga, silence," Hood said right before he took his nine-millimeter and smashed it into Lonzo's jaw.

I could hear his jaw cracking like ice. It really sucked to be him. I watched his head slump over to his left shoulder as he fell unconscious from the pressure of the steel. Leslie sat and watched Lonzo take his beating with no emotion. The sight of her was making me feel some type of way. Talk about fake-ass bitches, she had proven herself worthy of the title.

"I been bringing you around family, in my house, and all the time you scheming with this nickel-and-dime-ass dude."

Hood had made Lonzo who he was. He had no real street cred before that. I mean he had killed some niggas for Hood and settled a few scores, but he was still a no one in the game where it counted. He had schemed his way next to Hood, making him believe he was who he needed by his side. Yeah, he had put in some loyal work, and with Hood being in a crunch for a right-hand man, he gave Lonzo a chance when really he should have given it to C-Lo, who had been with him forever. But C-Lo was young, wild, and crazy like O-Dog from *Menace II Society*. He just didn't give a fuck, so Hood had to keep him leveled.

"Bitch, I had to do something . . ." Leslie barked, shaking her head like she needed validation. "But it was never about you."

Those words surprised me. Confusion was all over my face. She focused her eyes on Hood, and for the first time I saw the hate in them. Leslie hated my husband and I never had any idea. How could I have missed that? She had played the game well.

"You came back from New York alive and . . . Rob didn't."

Her eyes burned a hole in Hood. Snot and tears ran down her face. She sniffed before going on. "Rob was all my son and I had. I begged him not to go with you. I tried so hard to get him to walk away from the dope life, your crew. What you call the Height Squad." She spat accusingly. "But noooo . . ." She shook her head from left to right. "He had to have your back, and look what that got him."

Now it all made sense. Her words surprised Hood. He never knew that she blamed him for Rob's death. Not once did she show any indication that she was bitter with him.

"You think that shit was my fault?" Hood hit himself in the chest with the flat part of his left hand. "Trick, what do you know? What you think you know? Rob was my nigga. I would have died for him. How about you?" He challenged her. "You really believe I took him to New York to be killed. Nah, the shit just happened. It's a price you pay in this game. That goes for me or anybody else in this life."

Hood turned to Lonzo, who was now conscious but from the look of things, still groggy. "And you, you two-timing-ass nigga." He pointed his gun at him. "You should know that, but you gone let a bitch trick you into stealing from me for revenge. Revenge that wasn't even yours, especially not for the price you gotta pay. Not so smart, brah."

"Man, fuck you," Lonzo managed to get out. His face showed his agonizing pain. He needed to be put out of his misery. I'm sure he even prayed for it.

"Nah, cuz you got fucked."

Lonzo's eyes bucked open at Hood's words. He tried to lift his head but couldn't. Hood pumped two into his chest and watched him slump over. For the first time, Leslie seemed shocked as she watched Lonzo suck in his last breath. I was sure this was her first time seeing anyone killed, but other than that brief moment of shock, she seemed to take it well.

I was in my own feelings while I watched the whole thing. I knew how Hood felt. When Leslie was grieving, I was there for her. Hell, Hood had been there for her, too. He had given her ungrateful ass a million dollars in cold cash to help her and Li'l Rob out. She had not only shitted on my husband, she shitted on me.

"I was down for you. I sympathized with you. I was your friend and you played me like a record. And that shit hurts."

"I didn't do shit to you that you won't get over. You have your husband and while you both live happily ever after, Li'l Rob and I suffer. Besides, Hood has plenty of money. This little shit won't put a dent in his big-ass pocket."

I know she didn't think that I was mad about some money. Clearly, this bitch was not from the streets, because if she were, she would've known better.

"Bitch, don't be stupid!" I yelled.

Her dumb words were getting next to me in ways that she did not want them to. For her to even still be talking to me, she had been given a pass, but she was so naïve it was ridiculous. It was time that I set her straight.

"Loyalty is priceless and betrayal gone cost you."

Leslie laughed when she heard my words. She still didn't get it. This was a game to her. "Mya . . . you are so full of shit, so fucking superficial. I can see straight through you. I always could. Look at what you did to your own so-called best friend, Rochelle. As for me, what are you going to do? Kill me?" She chuckled.

"No, I'm not going to kill you. I wouldn't do that. But he is." I nodded in Hood's direction and turned my back on Leslie as I said calmly, "Leslie, here is a lesson in loyalty. Hood, load that bitch up."

I walked away.

"Mya," Leslie screamed my name. Her scream

was immediately followed by two gunshots. I didn't have to turn back. I knew that Leslie was no more. And it was all because of her stupid decisions. Like so many others, Leslie had played with fire and got burned. Now Li'l Rob had to grow up without his mother. I know it sounded selfish, but in the game, you pay your consequences regardless of your current situation.

Four days after the killing of Leslie and Lonzo, Leslie's mom filed a missing persons report. Leslie's cousin Cynthia, who had been living with her, called my phone the day after the killing asking if I had spoken with her. She said that Leslie had not come home the night before and that her cell phone was going straight to voicemail. Of course, I told her that I not seen or spoken with Leslie in a few days. Cynthia was really worried because Leslie would never not call or come home to check on Li'l Rob. So she decided to call Leslie's mom, who had moved to Texas with her younger sister.

Leslie's mom caught the first flight out to Detroit to find out what was going on. The police department said they couldn't do anything because Leslie was an adult. But that changed when her car was found abandoned behind a gas station on the Southside. Now her face was flashing across the television screen as a missing woman. Hood and I sat watching the nightly news just to hear the story.

Hood's eyes left the television and landed

on me. I could tell that he was thinking the same thing that I was. This whole situation was crazy and did not have to happen. Leslie should have used her mind and not her heart. It had done nothing to help her, it only harmed her.

"Man, I'm still fucked up about your girl's betrayal." Hood referred to Leslie. "I mean Lonzo, that's another matter. The nigga was born a snake and would probably do anything for a come-up. I'm sure he welcomed her proposition. But your girl?" He shook his head in disappointment.

"Well, they both should have known better."

"That's a fact," Hood agreed.

I could tell that he had more on his mind. It bothered him that Leslie accused him of being responsible for Rob's death.

"Rob was my nigga when it came to the job. He was loyal in every way it takes to make it in the streets. I respected him for that. That's how we became cool beyond the work. On the trip to New York he told me that he was about to walk away from the game. And you know why? For Leslie. He wanted to make her happy. He said he was tired of them breaking up because every time she moved out, she took Li'l Rob with her and he wanted them to be a family. Rob said that right before the trip, she had gotten mad and left again, but she came back and begged him not to make the trip. The only reason he had come was to have my back and tell me about his plans. When he got out, he was going to buy more houses and rent them out just like the ones he already had. But he knew the risk, ain't no promises in this game."

My heart ached for Hood. He had a look on his face that said he needed to convince me. There was no need, though. I had his back and I knew his heart.

"Babe, you don't have to think about that no more. It was not your fault and what is done is done. There is not one thing you could have done that would have changed anything."

"No doubt. That's my point. Some people just don't understand what the game is all about. The rules are easy and clear-cut. Emotions can never be involved, unless you want to be fooled or dead."

I loved the way he summed it up. He didn't leave nothing out. I understood the game. That's why I wanted Hood out.

"I guess you can say that Leslie broke all the rules, then. She should have never crossed us. I mean what did she think would happen? Did she really think she could get away with what they had done? Was she that fuckin' stupid?"

I felt some type of way just thinking about it. Hood stared at the television. I'm sure he was thinking about what I had just said. Neither one of us would never fully understand Leslie's betrayal. Her actions were motivated by emotions that she could not control. It was because of those actions that her family and son would now suffer from her absence. I guess part of it was my fault. I should have never let her in my circle so easily. Nevertheless, I would never regret what had to be done to correct her actions. The only regret I had was that Li'l Rob would not have his mother around to see him grow up.

Chapter 33

"Hey." I answered Hood's call as I sat at a red light down the street from the salon. I was on my way in and my first appointment for the day was Ma. She had called and said she needed her hair done. I always jumped at the chance to hook her wig up.

"Look, I got to fly out to Miami ASAP to handle some business. I'll be back in a couple days."

I was worried, as usual. Miami? Those D boys down there were no joke: they be killing for five bucks. I did not want my husband out there.

"Hood, you know I don't want you go. And why all of a sudden? You know I hate that shit even more. Last minute setups," I whined.

"Babe, I promise it's legit. Everything's cool.

Me and C-Lo gone make this run and be back before you know it. Don't sweat it. Our flight leaves in an hour, so I got to get in gear."

"All right, be careful. Hit me as soon as you touch down and if someone even so much as look, you betta bust a cap in their dome."

I meant every word. I didn't want him taking any chances. All I cared about was him coming back to me.

"I gotcha, babe."

Ending the call, I felt distant and unsafe. I would not be satisfied until he returned. But for now I could not do anything about it, so I decided to go about my day as normal. I stashed my worry away. It would do me no good here in Detroit.

To my surprise, Ma was early. "It's about time you showed up." She smiled.

"Ma, you tried it." I returned her smile. "Don't be trying to say I'm late."

"Girl, now you know you ain't never been good with time. But I still love you," she joked. "No, I'm just early because I woke up this morning and made your dad breakfast. So instead of lying back down, I just decided to go ahead get dressed and head over here."

To hear her say she made Dad breakfast warmed my heart. I loved knowing that they were happy.

"Speaking of Dad and breakfast, how are things since you have been back at home with him? I mean, I know I hardly hear from you anymore." I grinned.

"Everything has been good. He is doing a

lot better. He is home more often, so now we have time to go out to dinner and catch a movie. Oh, we even go on long walks in the park and feed the birds. Things we used enjoy doing long before our lives went haywire. I had missed those simple things so much."

"Awww, Ma, you gone make me cry. I am so happy for you. I can see the smile on your face is coming from deep within. That is true love. You and Dad have something special. There are not a lot of long-lasting relationships anymore like in the olden days. You and Dad symbolize that they do still exist. I want that for me and Hood."

"And you will have it. Hood is a good man with values. He didn't just marry you because you were beautiful. He married you for love and I promise you that love lasts."

"So where is Dad now?"

"He went to see his PO today. They are making him attend some class. I think it's just something they use to make them pass time."

"Okay. I just want him to comply with that PO because he seems like an asshole," I commented from my own judgment.

"Yeah, that's what I been telling your father to make sure he goes. Oh, and another thing, he has been receiving these strange calls." Ma raised her eyebrow in curiosity.

"Strange calls? From who?" I wondered.

"I mean his cell rings and when he answers it, he claims that it is the wrong number or it's a hang-up."

"Well, what makes you think they are strange?"

"I don't know. Well, for one, the number is always private, and just the look he has on his face when he answers."

"Hmmm." I pondered over what she had said.

"You know, Mya, I could just be overreacting. I just thought that they were strange, but he says everything is cool, that his cell number just sucks and he might get it changed. But you know me. I like to worry." She shrugged it off.

I could indeed verify that she was a worrier, but at the same time, I didn't want to blow it off. Maybe I would pull him aside and talk to him about it.

"Other than that, everything is cool." Ma finished up what she was saying. "On another good note, he just booked us a flight and in a couple of weeks we are going to Hawaii."

"He did?" I was surprised. "Wait what about his PO? He will need to get approval to leave the state."

"Already taken care of. He said once the travel agent got all the paperwork together, he took all that down to his PO and he approved it."

"Okay, now that's what's up, Dad on top with his stuff." He was pulling out the stops to get his lady back.

"Yes." Ma grinned from ear to ear. She was ecstatic. "I told you he was stepping up his game."

"I see. Go Dad!" I chanted. "Oh, and we have got to go shopping, and I don't want to hear no excuses. You have to be fly every day."

"Mya, don't start! I'm not spending hours in one store. Now maybe we can pick up a few things, but that's it."

She agreed, but made sure to set her ground rules. This was one lady who despised shopping. Don't get me wrong, she loved nice things, she just did not have patience to look for them. So she sent Monica and me out to shop for her instead, but this time I was making her come along.

"Ma, you have to have a bikini."

"Girl, I am not putting on a bikini and shame the devil."

"Ma, don't play. Your body is still banging. You wearin' a bikini."

Those were my ground rules. I had to admit, we had good genes. Ma was in her forties and her body was still tight and firm. Her weight was still the same 120 she weighed ten years ago. The lady didn't even go to the gym and she still had a six-pack. But she did eat pretty healthy and being a nurse kept her active. She was proof that you did not have to be a celebrity to be forty and fabulous. Dad was going to have to fight off men in Hawaii with a stick.

"We'll see how it goes when we go shopping," she agreed.

"Cool, I will call Monica up and let her know when, so she can come along."

"Speaking of your sister, I'm meeting her for lunch today. I planned to tell her then."

"That works."

"You know, I'm still worried about her. Do you know I almost had to beg her to go to lunch with me? I think that damn boy is over there holding her hostage or something."

I had the same concern. He was always answering her phone and that annoyed the hell out of me. I had made up my mind, though, the next time he tried to blow me off, I would be heading straight to their crib. But for now, I just wanted to ease Ma's mind because I didn't want her to worry.

"Don't worry about it. I personally went by Ripple Turn and had a heart-to-heart with Rich. I made sure he understands in no uncertain terms that he is not to be putting his hands on Monica."

"Well, I hope he listens, because the next time I will be telling your dad about it. I can't continue to hide my concerns about this."

"I know, Ma. I can promise you if it happens again, shit gone get crazy for his ass. He's a punk anyway. He ain't ready for my wrath, or Hood's, for that matter. I been holding it back from him also because I know how it would go down. He would catch a bullet, simple as that. Monica acts like she so in love with him until it turns my stomach."

"I been trying to figure this mess out. I can't believe that she would put up with this. There was never any violence in our household. Your dad didn't ever beat me or talk to me crazy. So why she thinks this mess is okay is a complete mystery to me."

"I know, Ma. I thought about that already. All Monica does is denies the fact that Rich has touched her. Not once has she admitted it. But like I told her, she has Imani to think about. So regardless, if she wants to keep him safe, it ain't gone happen. He has been warned."

"I agree. I want them both away from him. I mean, as much as I want to keep your dad out of prison for beating the hell of Rich or worse, I will not stand back and allow him to push Monica around. Now she may be in love or blind to his bullshit, but we are not."

"Like I said, Ma, don't you worry about anything. It will be okay. Tell her about the shopping and make sure she understands that she will be going. So unless she wants to see me act a fool, she betta control Rich."

"Will do. Now can we get my hair beat so I won't be late meeting your sister?" Ma sat down in my chair and I prepped her to be styled. Two hours later, she was looking in the mirror admiring the big curls that I had put in her head. And it all belonged to her, no Brazilian hair anywhere. Like I said, the lady was fabulous. It would be no question to anyone when she walked out of this salon that her hair was indeed snatched and I would be to blame.

Chapter 34

I was finally heading home from the salon. The entire day had been crazy busy. It seemed like all of our clients had scheduled an appointment today, for whatever reason. I had done seven sew-ins myself and that didn't include the other four heads I colored, cut, and styled. Trina did double the clients I did, including some braids. Secretly, I prayed for her because she looked as though she might pass out on the way to her car. Poor Nora said she had arched so many eyebrows that she didn't care if she saw another one in her life.

But as tired as we were, we had tag-teamed it and all of our clients were happy. That made it worth it. But for now, I could not wait to get home to shower and slide into bed. That was going to be the highlight of my day. I hit the interstate en route to my house and thanked God that traffic was light. I would be home in twenty minutes. Talk about small miracles. The radio was on Sirius XM channel 47. When Tamar's "All the Way Home" came on, I turned up the volume and started to relax to the lyrics.

Then my stupid cell phone started to ring. "Ugh, can I ever catch a break," I said aloud. Someone always had to bother me when I was in calm mode. Damn. Instead of looking at the caller ID, I hit talk. Before I could say hello I heard crying. At first I didn't catch the voice.

"Who is this?" I asked, trying to level the phone on my shoulder. I needed to plug the phone into my car phone speakers. Once I connected the cord, I heard the whimper again.

"I'm sorry, so sorry. Please forgive me."

The voice was a whimper, but it was clear. I knew exactly who it was. "Rochelle," I said.

"Yes, it's me. Mya, I am so sorry for how I have behaved. I am such a horrible mother, daughter, and friend." She continued to cry as she accused herself.

"Rochelle, what is wrong? Are you okay?"

Her well-being was my only concern at this point. For whatever reason, she had decided to call me and I was glad for it. I thought nothing of her past mistakes.

"I'm okay. I'm fine, or at least I will be once I get myself back together," she sniffed. "I did it. I left Kalil."

That was music to my ears. I wanted to scream "thank God" but I contained myself. I just wanted to listen because she needed someone to do that. And she had called the right person, her best friend. But as I listened, I thought I heard what sounded like traffic in the background.

"Where are you?"

"I'm at a tire lube place sitting outside on the curb in the parking lot. I don't have my car."

I knew right then that that asshole Kalil was somehow involved and on some bullshit. But I would find out more about that later. Right now, I had to find my friend and make sure she was safe.

"What's the address?"

As Rochelle told me the address, I typed it into my GPS. I put my foot on the gas pedal and stabbed out at top speed. The address that she had given me was not far from Kalil's house. The neighborhood was not bad, but it was dark outside. Being a woman and alone at night was not good in any part of Detroit.

As I pulled into the Tire Lube Express parking lot, I saw a scared Rochelle sitting alone on the sidewalk with her knees up to her chest. I had never seen her so vulnerable. As soon as she noticed my Mercedes stop, she stood up and walked over. I hit the button to unlock the doors and Rochelle climbed inside.

"What happened? Why you are out here alone?" I knew what the answer was, but I wanted to hear her say it.

"That fucking Kalil! I have been telling him for the last couple of days that I was thinking about going home. I told him that I could not do it no more. I needed to be with my baby. At first he acted like it was cool, but then I told him I couldn't be with him once I left and we needed to go our separate ways. I mean, it was no love there anyway. He was just my escape from reality. I thought we were good. But when I got up today and said I'm leaving, suddenly I couldn't find the keys to my truck. I mean I searched that damn house high and low for four hours, still no keys. I guess he thought that would keep me there. But no, I said fuck him and I was going to leave anyway. Then he gone try to block the door and push me. Now, Mya, you know I'm crazy. I went ham on his ass. Right now, he got a busted lip and nose. And I broke up about five thousand dollars' worth of shit. Watches, some hand-crafted lamps he had . . ." She shrugged her shoulders as if it was nothing. "I been told him don't ever fuck with me." Rochelle could be ruthless when she was mad. If he didn't believe her then, I bet he did now.

"Well, don't worry, you can get your truck back."

"I know. I already called the tow guy, Pete, over at Hall's Garage. You remember him, don't you? He was Li'l Lo's uncle. He on his way over there now to pick it up. I will get the key, locks, and ignition changed by the dealership. I don't know why Kalil just would not let me leave. I told him that I had to detox, that weed shit is not for me. I was smoking from the time I got up until I went to bed."

"Oh, so you only smoked weed with him?" This was good news. I was afraid he had her on that white. I was glad to be wrong.

"Hell, yeah! What did you think I was smoking?"

"I was worried because I heard he sold that white and that he was on that shit, too. So I thought that's what he had you on, especially with the changes in your behavior." I had to keep it one hundred.

"No, Mya, I only smoked weed and drank hard liquor. That's why I was always out of it. The more I wanted to stop smoking, the more he encouraged it. But I was tired of being high out of my mind because when I closed my eyes, all I could see was Tiny. My baby needs me, Mya." She started to cry again.

"I know, but don't worry, you made the first big step." I reached over and embraced her and tears flooded my face as well.

"And Mya . . . Oh, my God! I am so sorry for how I treated you. The things I said to you were just awful. I was just hurt and you were the only person I felt that I could blame. I'm sorry. I love you and I know you were only trying to be there for me."

"It's okay. Don't worry about that right now. I know you were trying to grieve. The hardest part for me was walking away and staying away. But I prayed and they didn't go unanswered, you are here now." I wiped tears. "Now, I'm going to take you home with me for the night, get you a good hot bath, and into bed. Then tomorrow you can go get Tiny and go home."

"All that sounds like a plan to me," she agreed.

Throwing the car in drive, I slowly pulled

out of the parking lot; now I was homeward bound.

As tired as I was, I could not believe how my day had ended. Never in a million years did I think I would be getting a call from Rochelle tonight. But here she was in my car headed to my home with a plan already laid out to get her daughter back and clean up her act. Mrs. Wynita would be ecstatic.

Chapter 35

The next few weeks were great for everyone, Rochelle especially. She was now receiving therapy to help deal with the losses of Li'l Lo and Todd. She admitted that she felt like every male in her life left her in death, including her father, who had been dead for years now, and she just had not dealt with it. But she was doing well in her sessions. Mrs. Wynita had also joined her in therapy. They wanted to make their mother and daughter relationship stronger. Rochelle and Tiny were back at home and getting back into their daily routine. Our friendship was back to normal, too. We finally sat down and talked through it all. She forgave me for not telling her about my involvement with Squeeze, which ultimately led to Todd being gunned down years later. Even though the bullet was meant for me, she agreed that Todd being shot was out of my control.

She was back at work at the salon and all the girls were happy. We were back to our old ways, having fun and loving it. Rochelle apologized to Nora for the way she had cursed her out and treated her and Nora happily accepted. She understood completely that Rochelle was a totally different person back then. Now they were cool as a fan. They stayed at each other's booths talking up hair ideas. I playfully threatened them about slick trying to become besties.

We were at the salon enjoying ourselves for a bit before we opened the doors. Nobody had an appointment for like two hours, so we shut the doors and pigged out on the pizza that I had ordered for our lunch.

The new application to the hair show in New York had arrived the day before, so Trina and Rochelle were busy filling it out. I couldn't help but think that it was fate that the opportunity to apply had come around again. We missed it the first time around, but because of some screwups they reissued applications for contestants to sign up. And it could not have come at a better time, since Rochelle was back.

"We 'bout to go back to New York and kill 'em," Rochelle boasted.

"No doubt!" Trina cheered her on.

"I got some new styles in mind that I been workin' on. Them bitches betta slide back." Rochelle loved to talk trash. I laughed.

"I'm ready. They already know they in for it so we gotta go in and lay it out."

"Yep and afterwards . . . turn up, turn up!" Trina chanted.

"I know, right. Man, it went down last year. Nora, I'm tellin' you, you gone enjoy it."

Nora was all teeth. She was ready to go.

"Nora, like I said earlier, I want you to focus on the makeup. I promise they won't know what hit them. Our A game gone be super stupid."

I could not wait. They think we beat them last year. This year, we were simply going to blow minds and break the hearts of the competitors.

"Pam, you can go ahead and book the rooms. You know we're staying at the best, the Ritz."

They already knew that room and board was on me. Heck, the whole trip was on me. The only thing they needed money for was shopping; everything else I funded. All they had to do was worry about doing hair, winning, and having a good time.

My cell phone started ringing. It was Monica telling me that she was outside. As I got up to unlock the door for her, I noticed how full I was. I had eaten four slices of supreme pizza.

"Dang, Mya, what took so long?" she complained, just to give me a hard time.

"I couldn't walk fast. My stomach is about to burst from all that pizza." I rubbed my stomach and squinted my face to show how uncomfortable I felt.

"That is what you get for being greedy."

"Oh, shut up. We all in the back." I pointed and Monica headed in that direction.

"What's up, Rochelle?" Monica spoke and

headed straight to Rochelle and they hugged each other tight. It had been a minute since they had talked or been able to hang out.

"I swear, every time I see you, you are more grown up," Rochelle commented. "Mya, you remember when she was nothing but a bugaboo always tryin' to hang around us and give us no space?"

"Yep, I remember." I laughed. "Ugh, I used to want to just lock her in the room."

"Forget both of you. Ain't nobody wanted to hang around y'all," Monica teased. "That's why I turned out the good kid because I stayed out of you two's company."

"Ha, ha," I giggled.

"It's good to have you back, though, Rochelle. We missed you," Monica said sincerely.

"I missed you all, too. Now I'm back and ready to give all of you the business," Rochelle joked. "I already know it ain't been turnt up around here since I been gone."

"So what, are you calling me boring?" I jumped up. "'Cause I'm always turnt up! Turn down for what!"

"Now you all know her definition of turn up in here." Rochelle grinned.

"Yep, put the inventory away," Pam chimed in, and we all laughed.

"Whatever, haters." I laughed.

"Well, look, why don't we all go out to the club and celebrate Rochelle being back," Monica suggested.

I thought her idea was on point. We needed a ladies' night out.

"I'm game," Trina replied.

"Me too. It's been a minute since I been out with my girls. I miss the hell out of it. Oh, and wait . . . now when did you start clubbing, little Ms. Monica?" Rochelle put her hands on her hips.

"Oh, I forgot to tell you that Li'l Miss over here is a clubaholic now. She can't stop, won't stop. I told you that she dates Rich, that new guy that owns the Ripple Turn now," I reminded Rochelle.

"Yeah, you told me about that. Hmmm, well, I guess if your man owns a club, you have to be all up and through there." Rochelle snapped her fingers and we all laughed.

"You betta know it. Let them females know he's taken. 'Cause they be on him," Monica chimed. I liked to see my sister happy, but I wanted to say another female could have his ass. But I chilled.

———◆———

Saturday night was club night and we all showed up. It was me, Rochelle, Trina, Pam, Nora, Monica, Hood, Rich, and Hood's crew. We were ready to turn up and that's just what we did from the moment we hit the door. Rich pulled me aside when I first got there to apologize if he had offended me in any type of way and to assure me that he loved Monica. I told him that it wasn't the right time for that type of conversation, because I came to enjoy myself and celebrate my girl Rochelle.

Future's "Neva End" blasted out of the speakers and Hood pulled me to the dance floor. We were moving to the beat and really enjoying ourselves. I was glad that his spirits were up. Whatever business he attended to in Florida had worked out. It had to do with his missing money that Lonzo had been taking to Miami to clean up. He got it back, but he also locked in on another project. There was always tons of money to be made and Hood made sure he made it. I didn't care about money, but his success and loyalty made him happy. But only because it secured his family future. So I did my best to respect that. Hood held me tight and kept his face buried in the crease of my neck. That was one of his favorite places to be when we were close.

"I love you so much," he said as kissed me softly on my neck, then cheek. Those kisses led to my lips and the kiss was so passionate a tear ran down my cheek.

"I love you, too," I mouthed when our kiss unfortunately ended. The song ended and we went back over to our friends.

"Dang, Mya, all that kissin', y'all may as well get naked," Rochelle joked as we sat down, and the girls started laughing.

"Shut up with your nosy self." I blushed. "Y'all ready to go hard? Let's get on the Jell-O shots," I shouted.

"I'm with that," Monica chimed in. "Bartender, Jell-O shots all around!"

When I saw another bartender headed to Hood's table with that Don Julio, I knew it was over. Those Don Julio shots would put him down for the night. But I know my husband, his motto is "go hard or go home." He looked at me and winked. He knew exactly what I was thinking.

We were on one after we tossed back a few Jell-O shots. The dance floor became our mission and the DJ didn't let us down because Yo Gotti's "Act Right" came on.

"That's my shit!" Trina yelled and started twirling her hips.

I knew she was krunk because she didn't dance much. We were doing our thang on the VIP dance floor when Rochelle looked down and saw Kalil. I was so engrossed in the dance and song I almost missed him.

"Look." Rochelle tapped me on the shoulder and pointed down.

I followed her finger and there he was with his eyes glued to VIP and Rochelle. I knew he didn't want to start anything because his ass was not crazy, but I also didn't want Rochelle to go ham on him because she still felt some type of way about him taking the keys to her truck.

"Rochelle, just ignore him," I encouraged, praying that she listened to me because it did not take much for her to pop off.

She rolled her eyes in his direction then turned back to me with a huge grin. "Oh, trust me. I plan to. I wouldn't give his burnt-out ass the satisfaction."

Just then Rich, out of all people, walked up to Kalil and shook hands with him. Now that surprised me. I had no idea that they knew each other.

"Hmmph, you know they cool, right?" Rochelle added.

Shaking my head, I replied, "I guess now I do."

Not that I gave a fuck, but sometimes you never know who knows who.

"Yeah, he came by the house once." Rochelle glared at Rich and Kalil.

That made me wonder if Monica knew they were cool, but I doubted it. Something like that she would have mentioned. I looked over at her and she was still dancing, smiling, and enjoying herself. I had to check it out, though.

"Monica!" I had to yell her name over the music. She looked up and I waved her over.

I pointed down in the direction of Kalil and Rich, who were still chatting it up. Monica followed my hand gesture with her eyes.

"You never told me that Rich knew Kalil."

Monica, who was still moving to the beat, shrugged her shoulders. "That is because I didn't know. Besides, Rich knows a lot of people because of this club."

Now that she broke it down that way, it made sense to me. How they knew each other had nothing to do with me, so I decided to dismiss it.

I turned to Rochelle. "Maybe Monica is right."

"Girl, I guess," Rochelle replied. "Who gives a fuck anyway?"

"Exactly." I laughed.

"Turn UP!" I yelled. I was ready to continue my fun.

The night turned out to be great. We did everything we came out to do. It was times like these that I missed the most. I even thought for a brief moment about Charlene. In my own way I missed her. Before her greed for money and power changed our friendship, we had fun together, and tonight just brought those thoughts back. Now I questioned if I had regrets about killing her. That question didn't linger long, though, because the reality was it was me or her, and me dying was not an option.

Chapter 36

"I am in for the rest of the night. I just picked up everything I needed from the store."

I was on the phone with Rochelle. It felt good to have her call my cell so we could just chat about our day or whatever we had going on. I missed that so much.

"You lucky. I am heading straight home as soon as I get out of here. Wynita is already at my house with Tiny. Girl, she cooked and everything."

"That's good. I know Hood gone enjoy his meal. It's been a minute since I made him dinner. Lately all we've been doing is going out to some restaurant or having the chef come by. But not tonight. My baby gone taste my home cooking." I beamed into the phone.

To be honest, I was also looking forward to cooking my own food. I could not wait to start.

"What all are you making, Hazel?" Rochelle joked, calling me the name of the maid that used to come on television way before our time.

"T-bone steaks, loaded baked potatoes, and broccoli. For dessert, I'm making a peach cobbler, oh, and French vanilla Blue Bell ice cream." My own stomach growled after naming off the menu.

"Damn, Mya, I think I'm comin' over there when I get off. That whole menu sounds like it's going to be bomb."

"I know. I can't wait myself. Anyway, I got to get all this stuff put away so that I can get dinner started. I'll call you later on."

"A'ight bet."

I slid a twelve-pack of Heineken beer that I picked up for Hood into the fridge. I opened the freezer side and put the Blue Bell ice cream inside. I could not wait to get a taste. It was my favorite vanilla ice cream from a container. Just as I closed the freezer door, my cell started ringing again. Had it been anyone other than someone close to me, I would have ignored it, but it was Monica. I always answered for family.

"What's up, chic?" I greeted.

The distress sound of Monica's voice was clear. I could tell she was crying and my heart dropped. "Mya, Rich flipped out on me today."

"What?" I screamed. "What the fuck happened?"

"I came home from school and he started in

on me about quitting again. We had been talking about it lately but I had not made up my mind. Ever since that conversation you and I had, I started going to class more often. Well, today he wanted an answer about when I was going to stop completely. Finally, I just told him that I wasn't going to quit and that made him furious. I had never seen him that way. The next thing I knew he slapped me, dragged me, and threw me up against the wall in the den. I fought him back. I was kicking and screaming. When I wouldn't stop screaming, he dragged me upstairs, threw me in one of the guest rooms, and locked me inside. I didn't know what to do."

Monica continued to cry, but I could tell she was trying to conceal it. It was almost like she was having a whispered cry. I sat on the phone in complete awe. I could not believe that I was hearing what she was saying. But in actuality, I was not surprised. I knew that bastard was a woman beater and I had tried to warn my naïve sister. Being angry was an understatement.

"Where's Rich at now?" I knew he was around somewhere; her whispers were a dead giveaway.

"He downstairs in the kitchen fixing me lunch. He came up about twenty minutes ago apologizing and to let me out of the room. I told him I was hungry and so he went downstairs to fix me something. As soon as he was out of sight, I grabbed my phone to call you."

All of a sudden I thought about my niece. If he had touched her in front of Imani, he was dead for sure. "Where is Imani?" I screamed so hard my phone vibrated.

"She is with Ma. She stayed the night over there." Monica's voice was trembling. That punk-ass nigga had some nerve doing this to her.

"I'm on my way."

I hung up before she could say anything else. I didn't need words. I almost picked up the phone to dial Hood but I decided against it. He was dealing with a lot on his end. I would go get my sister on my own because I was not scared of Rich. I would blow his punk ass away in one minute flat. I headed to Hood's man cave where he kept all of his heat locked up. I reached for the piece that would make my point if need be, a sawed-off shotgun. I rubbed my fingers over the metal, admiring its stability and security. Grabbing the keys to the Range Rover, I headed out of the door. I guess Hood's steak dinner would be put on hold.

I raced top speed to Monica's crib. I had all types of thoughts running through my mind. Why had I given in so easily to Monica moving in with Rich? It was my fault. I should have just forbade it and made her hate me. But no, I wanted to give her a chance to be an adult, and now look what was happening. Pulling into their long driveway, I threw my Range into park, turned off the ignition, grabbed my gun, and walked top speed up to the door.

Not caring if the whole neighborhood heard me, I banged on the door like I was Five-O. I was sure someone would call the cops on me. I had my shotgun in full view. The door swung open and Monica was standing behind it instead of Rich.

Rage flooded me. The left side of her face was swollen along with her top lip. It was even worse than I had imagined or she had described. I was ready to pop a cap in Rich for sure.

"Tell him to get his punk ass out here right now!"

The entire time Monica had her eyes on my left hand where the shotgun was. She knew what I was capable of.

"He's not here. I think he was eavesdropping when I was talking on the phone with you." She didn't take her eyes off of the gun.

The fact that he was gone disappointed me, but it probably was best for him. "Get your shit!" I didn't mean to scream at her, but I was heated as fuck. I stepped inside the house as if I owned it. My vision was clouded by the tears forming in my eyes. I blinked several times trying to clear them. Now was not the time. I need to get Monica out of here for good.

"Okay."

Monica finally took her eyes off the gun, turned and headed down the huge hallway at top speed until she reached the stairs. I followed her with my gun in tow, ready for anything. At the edge of the staircase there were two Prada bags. I reached down and grabbed them both.

"Hey," I said to get her attention. Monica turned on the steps and faced me. "I'm going to take these out to your Charger."

"Cool." Monica turned back around and started racing back up the stairs.

Before going to Monica's car, I walked over to my truck and laid the shotgun on the front seat, because tugging the gun and the bags were too heavy. Afterward, I walked over the car and started loading the bags inside. Just as I was about to close the trunk, I heard Monica scream. I raced back inside the house and up the stairs.

"Leave me alone," Monica screamed.

"Monica," I screamed out her name.

I was halfway up the stairs when I remembered that my gun was outside in my car. I ran back down the stairs to retrieve it. Monica was no longer screaming and the silence bothered me, so I ran faster.

By the time I made it upstairs, Rich was standing in their bedroom in front of Monica holding her back. She was trying to break free but his grip was tight. He only glanced in my direction because he was more focused on containing Monica.

"She ain't leaving, so why don't you just go home. We were just having a little family disagreement."

"Bitch-ass boy, you betta get your hands off my sister and I mean now!" I yelled as I put the shotgun to the back of his head. He froze. "I told you about hitting on my sister."

"Mya, wait." Monica glued her eyes to the gun again. "Mya, please listen to me . . . don't do this. He ain't worth it," she begged.

With my finger on the trigger, my thoughts

were telling me to ignore her and shoot him. I could feel Rich shaking. He was scared and that gave me pleasure.

"Look, I love her. I just lost my head for a minute. But I can promise you, on my life, it will not ever happen again."

He was such a punk. I could see why he liked to push women around.

"I know it won't, because you better stay away from her. Keep your distance, or the next time this shotgun will go BOOM!" I yelled and pushed the shotgun into the back of his skull, making him jump forward with fright. I almost laughed at how scared he was. The only reason I didn't shoot him was because of Monica. I knew that deep down she cared for him.

"Get the rest of you and Imani's stuff and let's go!"

Monica grabbed two huge Burberry suit-cases on wheels. She had three Burberry carry-on bags to go with that. She put one of the bags on top of a suitcase and I grabbed the other two and leveled them in both my hands.

Monica led the way as we exited her room, but she stopped abruptly and reached into her front right pocket. She pulled out keys to the truck that Rich had given her and to the house. She turned to face him and tossed them at him. He stepped back to keep the keys from hitting him.

We made it to the top of the stairs before Rich finally found the courage to come out of the room.

"Come on, Monica, baby," he begged, sounding like a wounded puppy. "You know I love you. You, me, and Imani are a family."

I wanted to throw raw stinking onions at him. Monica paused at the edge of the staircase and slowly turned and looked up at Rich. Without saying one word, she turned back around, placed her hands on her suitcase handles, and walked away.

I was proud of her. I turned to Rich with my face screwed up like I smelled something foul. I had a few words for him. "Stay the fuck away from my sister." I hoped he listened.

Chapter 37

I put Monica up at the Hilton Hotel downtown. I had to keep her out of sight from Hood. Had he gotten a glimpse of her swollen face, it would have been over for Rich, and as much as I wanted to see his ass on a platter, I knew Monica would not want that and might even resent us for it. Her face didn't take long to heal because I had taken her to the doctor and gotten her the proper medicine.

To keep Ma from seeing her and bringing Imani home, we told her that Monica had the stomach flu. Of course, she wanted to rush right over and take care of Monica, but we convinced her that it would be better if she didn't come around because we didn't want her to get sick and risk Imani catching it. Thankfully, it worked. But now that the swelling had gone down, Monica ached to see Imani. So I told Ma bring Imani and her things to my house.

Ma arrived right around the time that I told her we would be back from the store. Imani attacked Monica when she made it inside the house. Monica soaked up all the kisses she received from her only daughter.

"Hey," Ma spoke as she came into the kitchen and set down some Kroger bags. She had stopped by the store and picked up a few items that I needed for this special strawberry smoothie that Monica was always bugging me about making.

"Hey," Monica and I said in unison.

Ma had been wearing a smile from the time I opened the door and let her and Imani inside the house. Now that smile had faded. Her cheeks flushed red and her mouth was now tight around the edges. Imani climbed down from Monica's lap and started playing with the colorful rhinestone bracelet she had on her tiny arm.

With one stride, Ma moved across the kitchen to the table where Monica sat looking like a child who was in grave trouble. I could see the movement in Monica's esophagus as she swallowed what I assumed to be a throat full of nervousness.

"So he hit you again, huh? And don't lie to me." Ma was stern. The look on her face measured both anger and disappointment.

Instead of answering, Monica nodded yes.

Ma turned and looked at me for a brief second, then back at Monica. "You knew about this. Why you didn't say something?"

"I begged her to wait a couple of days," Monica threw in.

"Why wait? You may as well tell me. There ain't much you can hide from me and I won't find out."

"I just needed some time to myself to think."

"Well, I know you ain't going back. Heck no, you can forget about that. So he can just kiss your ass."

"She's going be staying here with me for a while," I confirmed.

"I don't know why you thought it was okay to stay with that bum for so long. But you betta stay away from him because I'm very close to telling your dad. He should not have to be in the dark about this. The only reason he doesn't know is because I don't want him to risk his parole. However, this is the last straw. Anything else goes down with Rich and it's a wrap. Bastard thinks he can put his hands on you." Ma was emotional. But I knew exactly how she felt.

"You don't have to worry, Ma. It's over. I promise you that." Monica was a kid again when she spoke. Reality had set in.

"Well, Ma, have you ate? 'Cause I'm about to cook these T-bones if you want to sit and eat with us."

It was time to change the conversation. Since we were all together, we might as well eat and have a few laughs before we were all separated again by the other parts of our lives that always seemed to be pulling us apart.

"No, I've been running around all day. I stopped at Wendy's and ordered some nuggets and fries for Imani around lunchtime. So hook me up."

"All right, I'm going to grill these steaks and sauté some veggies," I said as I heated up the griddle and prepared to throw the already marinated steaks on.

Then all of sudden Ma started smiling.

"Okay, now spill it, what you smiling for?" Monica asked. I turned to see her all white teeth. Something was brewing.

"I guess it's okay if I say something now. I wanted to wait until everything was settled but I swear I can't hold it any longer."

"Please, Ma, just tell us." She knew I was impatient. I wished she would just get to the point and skip all the verbiage.

"When I leave here today, your dad and I are going to look at rings."

She stopped talking but her grin was even bigger now. Monica looked at me and I understood why we were lost.

"Okay, you looking at rings and . . . ?" Monica said.

"Dang! Do I have to spell it out to you two? We are going to look at rings because we have decided to renew our wedding vows. The other night, your dad took me out to dinner, then the waiter brought me out an apple crisp cinnamon pie with French vanilla ice cream with a ring on top and your dad asked me to marry me again."

"He did what?" Monica jumped up with excitement.

"Yep, he sure did."

Ma's grin never swayed. I was sure her jaws

hurt. But I understood how she felt because tears were running down my flushed cheeks. After all they had been through, I knew their relationship was going to be all right. Monica and I wrapped Ma in a big hug.

Finally, we sat down to eat. While eating our steaks, we started to plan the vow renewal. Monica and I had all these fabulous ideas of how we wanted it. But Ma made it clear that she wanted to keep things simple. Their first wedding had been huge. This time around, Ma wanted it to be about her and her man. She wanted him to enjoy her and her him. No questions asked. While we were totally disappointed, we wanted to respect her wishes.

After dinner Ma hugged us both good-bye, told us she loved us, and headed out. We had enjoyed ourselves. But Imani was becoming restless. She had eaten her dinner, gotten full, and now she was ready to rumble.

"*SpongeBob*," she started to chant. "Watch *SpongeBob*," she continued.

We knew exactly what that meant. She was ready to watch one of her favorite shows. I got up and washed her hands and face.

"All right, let's go in the den and turn on *SpongeBob*."

"Okay." She smiled and looked at Monica. "Be back, Mommy."

"Go ahead." Monica smiled.

I reached for Imani's hand and we skipped off to the den, where I turned on *SpongeBob*. She could watch that stuff for hours and you would not hear a peep out of her.

When I went back to the kitchen, I found Monica loading the dishwasher. I was glad she was doing that because I was too full to move. Until I noticed Monica wiping away tears. She was in her feelings again. This situation with Rich was not easy for her.

"What's wrong, Monica?"

"Nothing, you know, same old thing. I was just thinking about what's going on with my situation. But I'm cool, though."

But I didn't want her to think about it. I wanted her to just move on. I knew that thinking only brought on the pain. "Monica, you can't be thinking about—" She held up her hand and stopped me.

"Mya, you can't protect me from everything. I know you love me and you want to, but you just can't. I'm a grown woman now, not some child." She looked at me hard before she took her hands and dried the wet tears that were covering her skin. She sniffed back pain.

"Let me say this." Her voice was almost a plea.

"Okay, go ahead."

"I knew that Rich was trying to control me from day one, just from the small things he did. But once I moved in with him, he promised he would do better. I had my doubts but I liked him so much and I really wanted to try. He acted as if he was a family man and I wanted that for Imani. I wanted her to have a father like we had. I know you remember what it was like before Dad went to jail."

The look in her eyes pleaded with me to

understand. Our dad was great. He loved us and was always there. Nothing came before his family. But that all changed in an instant. I also remembered that.

"But then, the hitting started. A push here, push there, and then next slaps to my face and jaw. Even though I considered leaving, I had fallen for him. He was gettin' next to my heart. It was like double jeopardy, but the hittin' was too much. I knew I could not hide that for too long. I almost resented you for accusing him of hittin' me because I knew you were right. I knew that I could not fool you of all people. It was just the last straw. I could not take it anymore; that was as far as I could allow it to go. That's why I called you, Mya. I needed you just like old times, my big sister always there to protect me. But then I got scared and wondered for a brief second, what if you didn't come get me. What if you blamed me for allowing this to happen, after you told me so many times before?"

"Monica, I would never leave you. I would never not come and get you. Regardless of what has happened in the past. I love you, you are my baby sister, my heart."

The tears would not stop flowing. I completely gave up on trying to wipe them away because it was no use. We hugged and cried for at least five minutes.

"Well, on a good note, Hood will be back tomorrow and we will let him know that you and Imani will be staying with us for a while."

"But you still haven't told him, right?"

"No, I did not. All he knows is that you walked out on him." I hated keeping this from Hood, but it was for the best. He would for sure put a hot one in Rich. "Now we just gotta hope he don't hear about it in the streets."

"I doubt it. Rich has this good guy image that he likes to keep up. There is no way that he will tell anyone that he hit his precious girl-friend. Then people might know that he is not perfect and sweet," Monica said sarcastically.

I just wanted to end any conversation of Rich before I went out and did what I was good at, but this time I would let life deal with him. Rich would get what was coming to him eventu-ally. I would just sit back and wait. Right now getting Monica restored to her normal life was my main concern.

"I just want you to focus on school and Imani for now. I don't want you trying to rush out and get a place. Okay?"

Monica shook her head in agreement; she was still a bit emotional. Imani ran back into the kitchen and stopped in front us. "Can you guys watch *SpongeBob* with me?" I couldn't do any-thing but smile my niece.

"We sure can," Monica replied.

We went back in the den and watched *SpongeBob* episodes back to back for the next two hours until we all dozed off. I woke up to Hood kissing me softly on the lips.

Chapter 38

Monica's name was flashing across my phone. I reached for it with my free hand. Right away I knew something was up when she started babbling. "Mya, can you call Ma and tell her that I can't meet her for lunch today?"

"Yeah, I can do that. What's up?" I asked as I swept up the hair from my last client.

"We were supposed to grab some lunch at the mall but I need to stay after school to make up some lab work. I've been trying to call her but something is wrong with her phone. I won't be able to call her back until after my next class and by that time I'm sure she will be on her way to meet me. So I was trying to let her know early."

"She has been having trouble with that phone. I keep telling her to go replace it."

"I know, but you know how your momma can be," Monica joked.

"Oh, so now she my momma? A'ight." I laughed. "But cool, I will keep trying to call her to let her know. Oh, and I'll be home late tonight. Hood and I are meeting for dinner."

"All right. Imani and I might be in the bed when you make it in, then. I'm tired already and it ain't nowhere near bedtime. But look, I got to go, it's almost time for my next class."

As soon as I removed my cell from my ear, Trina and Rochelle came in all excited and waving a piece of paper.

"What's that?" I asked, wanting to know what all the extra smiles were about.

"We got in!" Trina answered. "We going to New York for the hair show."

"That's what's up." I smiled. "Wait . . . did you ever doubt that we would get in? I mean they do know that we are the shit." I was being conceited on purpose.

"Damn right they do." Rochelle had my back. We complemented each other. That is exactly why we were best friends.

"You two are crazy." Trina laughed. "But you are right. We are going to go there and kick some ass, on that major!"

"Man, we gone turn up, just us girls. I simply cannot wait," Rochelle said.

When Rochelle said "just us girls," I got an idea. "I'm going to take Monica. A girls' getaway would be good for her. She would really enjoy it."

She had gone through a lot with Rich and now she was back on her real life stuff, trying to figure it all out. Nothing would be better for her than getting away and turning up with her friends and sister. I would tell her about it tomorrow. I'm sure she would not give me any hassle.

"Yep, I think so, too," Rochelle agreed, and Trina followed.

"Hey, what's up?" Hood spoke as he stepped inside the room.

Trina and Rochelle turned and spoke at the same time, "Hey, Hood."

I, on the other hand, had a surprised look on my face. I had no idea he was coming by. We were supposed to meet up for dinner. If it weren't for the huge grin he was wearing, I would have thought something was wrong. I met him halfway and we hugged and kissed just like always. We never had any problems being affectionate; we didn't care who was around.

"Whewww," Rochelle and Trina said at the same time as they exited.

"Babe, I thought we were supposed to be meeting at the restaurant."

"I know, but I couldn't wait another minute to see you. So I figured I would just pick you up and we can drive there together."

My man was so sweet and thoughtful; that was just one of the reasons why I loved him. If I had to write out a list, I could sit down and write a thousand things. I still had my arms wrapped around his neck, so I lifted back up on my tiptoes and kissed him again. He squeezed me extra tight. I wanted to say forget eating, let's go straight home and jump in bed, but I chilled because tonight I had him all to myself. The streets would wait.

"Okay, let me grab my stuff."

I was walking over to the cabinet where I kept my purse when Pam walked up.

"Mya, your dad's parole officer is out front again."

"Ahh, shit." I popped my lips. Whatever reason he was here was probably not good and I simply did not have the time. "Did he say what he wanted?"

"Nope. Just that he wanted to speak with you."

"A'ight, send him back," I told her. "Babe, it'll just be a minute."

"Cool. I'ma go back here and chill."

"Can I help you?" I didn't have any time to waste so I got straight to the point when the parole officer rounded the corner.

"Well, for starters, your father did not show up for his appointment today. Is he here?"

I hated this fucking guy. If he wanted to know if he was here, why didn't he ask Pam for him instead of me? He was so full of shit. He knew very well that my father wasn't here. I rolled my eyes.

"No, he is not here. He was off today." My attitude was apparent.

"Hmmm." He gave me a suspicious look and I seriously considered telling him to get his ass out of my salon. Instead I remained calm.

"If you see him or when you see him, tell him he needs to contact my office tomorrow or I'm going to violate him. This is his second time missing his appointment date. That type of behavior is not tolerated." He talked as if he was reprimanding me.

I gave him a forced smile with only half of my teeth showing and said, "I sure will."

The guy disgusted me. He weighed about three-fifty and he was no taller than five foot four. His skin looked like it had been bleached two-toned and he had all these baby moles all over his face. And to top it off, he wore some gold-rimmed glasses with huge bifocal lenses. He was a real creep.

As soon as he left my area, I grabbed my things and told Hood that I was ready to go. I filled him in on what was going during the ride to the restaurant.

"I just can't believe he missed another appointment," I said angrily.

"Maybe he got tied up," Hood said, but he knew better.

Dad just seemed to have a knack for doing him, but that shit was not going to fly. If he kept doing him, he would find himself behind bars again. I pulled my cell out of my purse and dialed his number. To my dismay, it went straight to his voicemail.

"Ugh. Then he has the nerve to have his damn phone turned off. He is really trying my patience today. I don't have time for this shit!" I yelled and tossed my cell phone back inside my purse.

"Babe, calm down." Hood glanced at me as he drove. "I tell you what. We will just swing by the condo when we finish with dinner."

I knew Hood was just trying to ease my mind, but I could not wait that long. I needed to see my dad immediately.

"No, go now." I sat back in my seat and folded my arms.

Hood turned the car around and headed in that direction without asking me one question. As soon as we pulled up, I noticed Ma's car outside in the parking lot but Dad's car was nowhere in sight. Sometimes he parked it in the garage, so I assumed that it was there. Hood knocked on the door when we made to their condo. After a round of extensive knocking, we concluded that they must be out.

"Ma's probably in the car with him."

"Did you try her phone?" Hood asked.

"Something is wrong with her phone. Monica was trying to reach her earlier and couldn't. Let's just go. We can stop back by after dinner."

"Whatever you want to do," Hood responded as we turned to leave. But suddenly my bladder was calling. I had to use the bathroom. I would have used before leaving the salon but that ugly parole officer had me all in my feelings.

"Babe, wait. I need to use the bathroom."

I started to dig around in my purse to find my key to the condo. "I promise it will only take a minute." I found the key and wiggled it into the keyhole.

"Damn, your moms got it cold in here," Hood said as he stepped inside behind me. I agreed with him: it felt like a freezer.

"I know. I'ma make it quick." I started down the hallway at a fast pace.

Hood said something, but I heard nothing. I grabbed my chest as the wind blew completely out of my body and I fell to my knees on the floor. Since my legs had given out on me, my mind told me to crawl. So I did. I wanted to scream but I had no vocals.

"Ma," I somehow managed. Her body was covered in her own blood. "Hood!" I screamed his name.

I heard Hood's footsteps as he ran down the hallway, but he stopped and hit the wall with a loud thud. I looked up at him and saw that his face was full of tears; they ran freely down his cheeks. Suddenly his gaze left mine and he froze. With a heartbeat well over two hundred and hands that would not stop trembling, I followed his gaze. To my horror, there were a pair of legs on the floor leading out into the hallway from my parents' room.

I jumped up and ran to those legs and found that they belonged to my dad. I dropped to my knees and lifted his head. "Dad, Dad, Daddy," I yelled. "Daddy, please get up. Please, Daddy," I screamed over and over again.

In the background, I heard Hood calling 911. This had to be a dream.

Chapter 39

I woke up in the hospital two days later. Apparently, I had been inconsolable. I kept passing out and was dehydrated. My world had balled up and crumbled right before my very eyes. I had experienced hurt in a way that I would never experience it again. I was numb. I was such a vegetable that it was left up to Hood to tell Monica that our parents, Lester and Marissa, were dead. Someone had killed them and left them lying in their own blood. Monica and I would never be the same.

Someone had ripped us at the gut and didn't think twice about pouring alcohol on an open wound that would never ever heal. Whoever had said that time heals all had lied. There was no amount of time that could ever make this okay and there was no convincing me otherwise.

I had always been the rock. I was the glue that held my family together. But this had taken its toll on me and I could not find myself. In my mind, I had been pushed off Mount Everest and I physically felt every bruise. But Monica stepped up. She, Hood, and Rochelle hit the pavement and started planning the funeral services. Hood had put his business aside completely. His family was in need of him.

On the day of the funeral, I was still weak from pure despair. I lost weight because the only thing I could manage to do was drink fluids. Hood had begged me to eat but I couldn't. The knot in my throat was so big there was no way food could get past it. I had lost ten pounds so quickly it brought tears to Hood's ma's eyes when she saw me. She had come to town as soon as she had found out and was helping out around the house. I really appreciated it because I couldn't do anything in the state I was in.

The day of the funeral was sunny and bright. Over two thousand people had showed up. My parents had known a lot of people and they all showed up to celebrate their lives. People stood outside the temple because there was not enough room to get in. The crowd overwhelmed Monica and me because we just wanted to be alone. When it was finally over, I had Hood take me home. I was in no mood to mingle. Monica said that she would go to the repast and show a little gratitude for those who had come out. Rochelle promised me she would take care of Monica, who I knew was trying so hard to be strong for me.

When we got home, I undressed and climbed into bed. Hood climbed in with me and wrapped me in his arms. He held me tight as I cried until I went to sleep. I found comfort in my dreams when I saw Li'l Bo, Ma, Dad, and Monica. We were all in our old apartment in the Brewster in the living room dancing to the O'Jays' "Love Train" just like we used to. Then I saw us out eating burgers. We laughed as we watched Li'l Bo bite off half of his in one bite. Then Ma looked at me calmly and told me that everything was going to be okay. I could feel her and it was so real, but then I opened my eyes and it was morning and that hurt so bad. The only reason that I didn't scream out in pain was because I felt the comfort of Hood, whose arms I was still wrapped in. At that moment, I remembered that I did have a reason to live. There was Hood, Monica, and Imani. Ma was trying to tell me that.

———⊙———

"Good morning sleepy head." Hood kissed me on my cheek.

"Hey you," I said, still a little groggy.

"Did you sleep well? I mean it sounded like you did. All that snoring," Hood joked.

"I do not snore." I smiled for the first time in almost two weeks. "But yes, I did sleep good."

"Good, I'm glad to hear that. Are you hungry?"

I should have figured that he would ask me that. It had been his number one question since I got home from the hospital.

"Yes, I think I'll eat something. Can you make me some eggs and toast?"

"Sure thing." Hood jumped up so fast that he scared me.

"Dang, babe, you okay?"

"Oh, I'm fine. I just want to make the food before you change your mind."

Again, I smiled. "Hood, just go and make the breakfast. I promise not to change my mind. I'm going to take a quick shower and I will be down."

"A'ight."

He hurried out of the room. I knew he was going to tell his mom to make it. And I was right: by the time I climbed out of the shower he was in the bathroom, washing his face and brushing his teeth.

I got a surprise visit from Big Nick after I finished eating breakfast. I had not gotten a chance to see or talk to him at the service so I was glad to see him.

"I thought that I would come out to check on you. The crowd was so thick yesterday it was hard to reach you." Big Nick walked over and hugged me.

"I know. I swear all of Detroit was there."

"Yeah, your mom and dad were well known. So I wasn't surprised," he confirmed. "How you are you and Monica doing?"

"We cool, just glad that part is over with. Monica still sleeping, she's been handling a lot lately."

"I know. I came by to see you when you were in the hospital. You better?"

"Yeah, I am, I just need to eat and stuff. And I am now, so I'm good."

"Okay." He half smiled but the look on his face told me that he had a lot on his mind. "I just want you to know that I'm gone take care of this. I vow with every inch of life I have in me that I'm going to find out who is responsible for this. And I swear whoever it is gone pay dearly with their life. I promise you that. So you rest easy and don't worry. If you or Monica need anything, you know how to get in contact with me. I'll be by in a couple of days to check on you two. Okay."

"A'ight." I had to wipe tears away.

Big Nick came over and hugged me again. "I love you and Monica, all right. You tell her that when she wakes up, okay."

"I will."

"And I'll be back."

"Okay." I sniffed. I knew he would be out pounding the pavement looking for who was responsible, but Hood was also already on that same job. I could not allow whoever had done this to continue to walk the earth. That was the ultimate no-no. Whoever they were would find out they had fucked up.

<hr>

A short two days later, Hood came home and told me that Big Nick had just been killed. Someone had shot him up in IHOP's parking lot. I simply could not believe it. Was Detroit really this fucking crazy? This town had to be cursed or I was cursed; either way this mess was insane. Who wanted Big Nick dead? My head was spinning on my shoulders. I started to wonder what Dad and Big Nick had been up to. Were the deaths related? I mean, what were the chances they would be killed so close to each other?

Before I could think this through, Monica strolled into my room and plopped down on the bed in front of me. I could tell that she had been crying. Hood had told her before me about Big Nick.

"Are you okay?" I asked, but I knew she was not.

"I have to leave Detroit," were the unexpected words that rolled off her tongue. I almost didn't know how to respond.

"Why? This is your home. You have never lived anywhere else."

I'm not sure if that was a good defense, but I had no idea of what else to say. But I would not say go.

"I know, Mya, but it's time for a change. I can no longer stay in this city. I feel like it's haunted, too much death. I just can't do it anymore. I want to just take Imani and go." Her mind sounded so made up.

"But you can't go. What about me? You and Imani are the only blood family I have. I can't lose you."

"I know."

We both started to cry and hug each other. At this point in our lives, we were almost helpless. There were so many unexpected twist and turns, and the road just seemed to be getting longer.

"What do you think will become of us?" Monica asked. "We have lost everything, our puzzle is so full of holes." Her description could not have been clearer. "First Li'l Bo and now Mom and Dad. I don't know, but I'm suffocating." Monica let out a cry from her soul. I held on to her for dear life. I loved my sister so much.

"Let me think for a couple days. I will come up with something, but we have to be in this thing together, we can't separate at a time like this. Me, you, and Imani must always stay together."

"Okay," Monica agreed, and I felt relief.

"Where's Imani?"

"She went out with Hood's mom. She said she was taking her to Chuck E. Cheese so that I could rest."

"Well, how about you go take a nap and I'll order up some takeout for dinner." Nodding her head in agreement, Monica got up and went to her room.

I slid on some gym shoes and headed downstairs to talk with Hood. I found him in the den watching television and having a beer.

"Hey, babe," he spoke as he sat up on the couch.

"I see you relaxing." I sat down next to him.

"Yeah, thought I'd watch the game and have a beer."

"Well, I hate to bother you, but I came down

to tell you that I need you to take me over to the condo. I want to pick up some things from there."

Hood looked at me like maybe he heard me wrong. "Uh, no, babe. I don't think that's a good idea."

"Hood, it's been almost two weeks. I will be okay. Don't worry."

He hesitated but finally he agreed.

———◆———

There was still some yellow tape on the door but the detective had called a couple of days before and said it was no longer a crime scene. Inside, I made my way down the hallway past the spot where I remembered Ma's body lying and then inside the door of their bedroom where Dad had lain. Their closet was my main target.

I wanted to retrieve a box that belonged to my father that Ma would never let me look inside of. I was feeling inside the closet on the top shelf, but I could not feel anything. After a few minutes of searching with no luck, I had Hood come and look for it. Before he located it, I was beginning to think that maybe the cops had found it, because I knew they had done an extensive search. After grabbing a few other things that I wanted to have, immediately I left. Everything else was going to be boxed up by Rochelle and Trina, who both volunteered to do so.

Chapter 40

I had gotten up early this morning. Rochelle had called to check on me and to gossip before heading into the salon. She said that she would be out to see me in two days on her off day. She wanted to talk about canceling the trip to New York but I told her no. My mind was made up, the show must go on.

We were still trying to get back into the normal swing of things, which was so hard to do. I had not been back to the salon yet. I just was not ready. But Monica said she needed to keep busy, so she decided to go back to school. Today was her first day back, so I got up and had breakfast with her before she left. Once she was gone, I decided to head back up to my room.

I told Monica during breakfast about me going by the condo the night before. I told her

that I had picked up a few things, including
Dad's box. Now the box was sitting on my dresser
and it seemed to be staring at me. I almost felt
like it was watching me back. It was rusty gold
with black circle specks all around it. The circle
specks seemed like eyes to me. I shrugged my
shoulders to brush it off. After a few more minutes of just looking at it, I walked over and
picked it up. I had to pry it open because I did-
n't have the key. After getting it open, I found a
journal, which I thought to be strange. Men
normally didn't have journals, but as I began to
read, I confirmed that it indeed belonged to my
father.

On the second page, Dad had written about
a guy named Harold Montgomery and some
threats that Harold had made. The handwriting
was messy and hard to read, but from what I
could tell, Harold's kids may have put a hit on
him. Because the handwriting was unclear, I
couldn't really get the full story. I hoped that
there would be more on another page.

As I flipped through a few more pages, something fell out. There was a date written on the
back of it in black pen. This particular date stood
out to me because that was the same date that I
had found my parents dead. I flipped it over
and realized that it was a picture. I had to do a
double-take when I looked at it because I knew
who the people in the picture were. It was confirmed when I looked at the bottom of it, where
the names were listed as Quad, Rich, and Montgomery.

Now my mind was racing. What the hell was

going on? Why were Quad and Rich in a picture in Dad's journal? Something was not right. I ran out of my room and raced down the stairs to where Hood was once again watching television. Since all this had happened he had refused to leave my side. I stood in front of him breathing hard from running down the stairs and I dropped the picture in his lap.

"Quad and Rich are brother and sister." That much I had figured out for sure.

Hood sat up and grabbed the picture from his lap. "What?" he asked, looking at it with his eyes bucked.

I started pacing the room, my hands going to my forehead. I wanted to figure out what was going on but my mind was jumbled. "I mean I don't know what makes sense anymore, babe. I was upstairs reading the journal—"

"What journal?" Hood now looked confused.

"There was a journal inside that box you got out of the closet."

"Oh . . ."

"I was reading the journal and Dad was talking about some dude named Harold Montgomery and threats from his past. It's not clear, but he also said something about Harold's kids having a hit on him. It's really strange—but then that fucking picture falls out and look at the names on it."

Hood looked at the picture again. "What the fuck!"

"That's exactly what I was thinking. Something is going on. Oh, and I found out from Rochelle this morning that Rich and Kalil are cousins. Babe, it's some weird shit going on." The more I thought about it, the more suspicious I got.

"Are you sure that's what Rochelle said?" Hood asked.

"Babe, Rochelle told me that she saw Kalil and Rich together the other day. She said that Rich asked her about Monica and she told him to fuck off. But then yesterday she was doing this chick's hair that knew that Rochelle dated Kalil and Monica dated Rich. The girl asked her if she knew that Kalil and Rich were cousins." I rested my case. "Something ain't right."

"Damn right, we gone get to the bottom of this shit. That's a fact."

Hood pulled out his cell phone. He started making a few calls while I sat down on the couch as my mind wandered.

"Look, I want you to hang tight. I need to make some runs to figure some shit out. I will call you when I get straight. Don't leave this house. Period," he stressed because he knew how I could be. "Promise me you won't leave, Mya."

"I promise."

All I wanted was a drink and I needed it now. I headed to the kitchen and pulled out my merlot. I popped open the bottle and watched as it landed in my glass. The first swallow calmed me to my toes. It felt so good that I thought about drinking straight from the bottle.

Chapter 41

Time was creeping by slow as hell. I literally thought that I could hear the ticking of my Guess watch. Sitting on the couch in the den, I turned the television to *The Waltons*, one of my favorite golden oldies shows, but I didn't hear one word of what was being said. Normally the show would have my undivided attention. Sometimes I wished their lives were mine. I was sure that I would be much better off. Instead, I was sitting on the couch with my mind wandering all over the place, but the merlot I was consuming was helping me to stay calm.

"Hey, auntie." Imani ran to me and gave me a hug and I really needed it. She and Monica had just made it in for the evening. I was getting so used to their routine that I almost didn't

want them to ever move out. I knew it would be
hard for me when the time came.

"Hey, sweetheart. Did you have fun at day-
care?" I kissed her on the cheek before she
could break free. She was a busybody.

"Yes, I played all day." She smiled and pulled
on one of the long braids that I had put in her
hair a couple days before. I enjoyed braiding
her hair because it kept my mind busy. It also
brought back memories of when I used to braid
Monica's hair. It was therapeutic.

"She should be tired, I know I am," Monica
said, still holding her backpack on her shoulder.
She looked tired, but school kept her from sitting around thinking about Ma and Dad. "You
look relaxed."

"I don't know about all that. Just sittin' having a drink to ease my mind."

"Have you been sittin' on this couch all
day?" Monica asked with concern. She tried to
encourage me to go back to work. Get back to
my normal routine, was the way she put it.

"Actually, no, I have been upstairs and in
the kitchen," I joked.

"Yeah, you look busy," she said sarcastically.
"Well, I'm going to feed Imani and put her in
the bed."

"No, Mommy, I don't want to eat." Imani
was rolling around on her Hello Kitty beanbag
as she pleaded. She was not an eater; she only
liked junk food or Apple Jacks cereal.

"Come on now, Imani, you have to eat something. I tell you what, if you eat a little I will give

you some vanilla ice cream for dessert," Monica bribed.

"Okay," Imani agreed once again. Monica had outsmarted her.

"Once I get Imani off to bed, I'll be back down to watch television with you and have some of that merlot. I need some to help me relax, too."

"Cool, I have another bottle in the kitchen. This one is about empty. I was going in."

While Monica took care of Imani, I contemplated whether I should tell her what was going on or not. Right now, Rich was a touchy conversation for her because she still had feelings for him. But I decided that I had no choice. After she shot Luscious, Monica made me promise to never keep something important from her again. And to be honest, I thought it would be for the best. Maybe she would see that letting him go completely was the only thing to do.

"Wheww! I finally got her to go to sleep."

Monica bounced on the sofa. She sounded exhausted, but I guess going to school all day and raising a toddler could do that, so I understood completely.

"I swear all your niece wants to do is watch *SpongeBob*! We are going to have to take her somewhere to meet him."

I smiled because I agreed. "Yeah, we can make that happen even if we have to rent him for her birthday or something," I said as I started pouring Monica a glass of merlot.

"Let's make that a plan, then," Monica agreed

as she reached for the glass and took a big swig. As it ran down her throat, a look of relaxation filled her face. "Now that is exactly what I needed."

"That is the same way I felt when I took my first swallow about four hours ago . . . Now I'm in there." I laughed.

Monica kicked her feet up on the sofa.

"So I wanted to talk to you about something. I know we still grieving and this just may add to it, I mean really I don't even know if it means anything yet, but I wanted to talk to you about it anyway."

The relaxation on Monica's face was now out of the window. I had officially ruined that for her. I felt bad about it but my choices were truly limited.

"Just say it." Monica didn't want to me to beat around the bush because any information we received was always a mess.

"Do you remember Quad, that chick I got into it with at the club that night? Well, I found out today that—"

"I remember," she interrupted.

"Okay. Well, I found out today that Quad and Rich are brother and sister."

"Huh?" Monica was confused and surprised. "How? I mean—" She stopped talking and threw up her hands.

"Look, this is all strange to me, too. But last night when I went to the condo I went for a reason. A while back Ma and I ran across this box that belonged to Dad. I wanted to look in it but Ma told me not to because it was Dad's personal stuff. Now I can't explain why, but last night it was on my mind to go get that particular box. So I went over with Hood, I found it, and I brought it back. Today I opened it and found a journal. Of course, I started reading it, and I found where Dad talked about some guy named Harold Montgomery. Apparently, they had some type of beef back in the day. Dad talks about threats and the man's kids and all that, but it is unclear."

"What does this have to do with Rich?"

"While I was looking the journal, a picture of Quad and Rich fell out of it. What is Rich's last name?" I asked her.

"Montgomery" rolled off her tongue in slow motion, or at least that was the way I heard it.

I closed my eyes for a brief second. "On the bottom portion of the picture the names read Quad and Rich Montgomery."

Monica eyes bucked out in shock. "I can't believe it." She sat her glass down. "So what is going on, Mya?"

"Monica, I wish I knew, but right now I don't know. But something ain't right. And guess what else? On the back of the picture was the date I found Ma and Dad at the condo."

Monica's eyes filled with water, and tears threatened to fall.

"Has Rich ever mentioned anything about Quad to you? She is always at the club."

Monica shook her head left to right. She tried to speak but the words didn't come out, so she cleared her throat. "No he never mentioned her, and all the times I saw her at the club he never said anything to her, or least I never saw it.

And as for his family, he never talked about them. He did tell me once that his mom had died when he was a kid, but he never mentioned his father. Oh, one time he did say that he had an older brother who lives in D.C., but they never talked on the phone or nothing in front of me."

"Hmmph," was my reply. That dude was hiding something, I could just feel it.

"But, Mya, now that I think about it, Quad and Rich do kind of look alike."

"You know, I was thinking the same thing when I saw the picture. That's how I knew they had to be brother and sister."

"Damn." Monica picked up her glass again.

"Oh, and another thing: I found out this morning from Rochelle that Rich and Kalil are cousins."

Monica looked at me long and hard, shook her head, and downed the rest of her merlot. "This is some bullshit," she said as she looked at her empty glass. "Do you think they had something to do with Ma and Dad's death?"

That was a hard question for me to even have to listen to, so I know the words burned coming out of her mouth.

"I don't know."

A tear slid down my left cheek. Just knowing they were gone brought bile to my throat but I breathed in deep and it went back down. The front door opened and closed as the alarm chirped, letting us know that Hood had entered the house. I kept it on twenty-four seven now. I also kept the cameras that we had outside of our home on. I didn't trust shit now, everyone and everything was suspect.

"Babe, I need you to go with me," he directed me. "Hey, Monica?" he spoke.

"What's up, Hood?"

He could tell by the look on her face that she knew. "I guess Mya told you what is going on."

"Yeah," Monica said softly. I knew she could cry at any moment.

"Well, look, everything is going to be okay. I want you and Imani to stay inside; don't go nowhere. I got alarms on every inch of this house. Cameras, too, so you are safe here. And you know where all the heat is."

Monica didn't utter one word. It was clear that she still needed to take all of this in. I guess it would be fair to say we all did. I quickly got ready and headed out with Hood.

During the ride, he never said one word. Something told me this was not good, but he had his prey. We drove to an abandoned house located outside of town. The house was located behind a wooded tree area, but it was separated from the trees. It was like a house sitting behind a lonely island. The house was not big, I could tell from the outside. I had never seen this place before but I recognized the all-black Dodge Challenger with dark tint and black rims that was parked out front. It belonged to C-Lo.

Hood got out and came around to my side to help get me out. He told me to watch my step because the ground was messed up. When he opened the front door, my heart sank. I'm not sure why, but the look of the place made me feel like I needed air. I turned toward the door and drank in as much fresh air as I possibly could. I turned back around and took in a full view of the room. Surprisingly, the hardwood floors looked as though they had been refurbished. It appeared as though the house only had one room, the one we were standing in. The room was not furnished and the walls were bare. There was an old stove in one corner that looked like it was from the 1930s and a rusty old Victorian tub that was welded to the floor in the other. One look at the tub and I realized that it was full of bloody water.

I finally turned my gaze to the middle of the room, where there were twenty-two-inch car tires stacked five tires tall. The stacks were lined up in a row of three, and tied to them were Quad, Rich, and Kalil. Just the people I needed to talk to. And by closely looking at the three of them, it became apparent to me that the blood in the tub belonged to Kalil. He was fucked up and his face was beaten almost beyond recognition.

I turned to look at Hood. He shrugged his shoulders. "Nigga wouldn't shut his mouth-piece. He understands now."

I looked back at Kalil. His head was swaying from side to side and blood was dripping out of his mouth and onto his clothes and the floor. That was annoying. I shook my head in disgust because he was being dramatic.

I could feel Quad's eyes on me. She had something to say to me, I could feel it. When she got her chance she did not disappoint me. "I'm supposed to be scared of this bitch!" she yelled. She wanted my attention, so I gave it to her. Her outburst intrigued me. I said nothing so she continued, sucking her teeth before going on. "Weak bitches get served on my block, A one day one."

She was obviously angry with me. "Is that what you want to do? You want to fight me?" I was ready. This bitch had disrespected me one time too many. Plus, I hated it when bitches played tough. If she thought I was weak, then she could get it. "Okay, Hood, untie this hoe!" I barked at him.

"Mya, that is not why we are here. Stick to the business at hand, fuck what she got to say." He tried to change my mind.

"Hood, untie her!" I looked at him and yelled. He was about to piss me off.

Instead of arguing, he gestured for C-Lo, who was standing over by the tub, to untie Quad. Quad kept her eyes on me while C-Lo undid her ropes. I could see the steam coming out of her ears. She could not wait to get her hands on me.

As soon as Quad was on her feet, she came for me. I ducked her punch, came back up, and punched her in the nose. Blood flew everywhere. Seeing the blood really made her angry; she yelled something that I could not make out and charged at me. I grabbed her entire face, pushed her back, and then kicked her between her legs. She fell to the floor.

I yelled, "Get up, bitch!"

"I'ma kill you, you stupid bitch!" she screamed.

"Bitch, bring it," I said calmly.

Again, she jumped up and charged for me. This time, I took my nine-millimeter and busted her in the face so hard that she spun around full circle then fell in the tub face forward.

"Is that what you want, bitch? I'm from the Brewster, now stop playing with me."

Quad slowly lifted her head out of the bloody water and swung it, causing the water to fly everywhere. She tried to speak but the only thing that came out was the gurgle of blood in her throat. C-Lo picked her up, dragged her back to the tires, and tied her back up.

I turned my attention to Rich. I hated the sight of him. "So I guess you forgot to tell Monica that Ms. Big Time Dope Pusher Quad here was your sister and that this weak nigga"—I pointed at Kalil—"was your cousin."

"Man, fuck that. I don't owe her shit. My business is my business. You motherfuckers are through, anyway." I could not believe his punk ass was trying to beef up at me. This was the wrong approach.

"No, from the looks of it, partner, you through." Hood pulled out his gun and shot Rich in his right knee. He screamed out like a girl and I almost laughed. "Respect my wife, nigga," Hood ordered.

Hood looked at me and said the words I wanted to know but didn't want to hear. "Babe, they did it. All of them. They killed your parents."

For a minute my heart stopped. I could not breathe and the room started to close in. I wanted to run outside for fresh air. This house was too small and evil was in it. The tears started. They ran all over me and there was nothing I could do to stop them. Memories of the past with my parents started crossing my mind. I wanted to shake them off so that the air would come back into my lungs. The thought of Quad made my blood boil. She had no idea who she had fucked with.

Hood came up behind me and started to rub my back. He gave me the strength that I needed to come back to life. Whispering softly in my ear, he reassured me that everything was going to be all right. Slowly, my heartbeat became level again and air filled my lungs.

I looked at Quad. She wanted my attention; now she had it for sure. I needed to understand why. "You did that? You laid a hand on my mom and dad? Was it you who decided to take them from me? You do know that my sister and I are alone now?" I spoke from my soul, which at this moment was a river of memories of my beloved family.

"So what? Your dad got what he deserved!"

I could not believe that she said that. The bitch had balls. Lucky for her they were not physically there. Because I would have cut them off and made her eat them. But I wanted to hear what she had to say. "Why? Why did he deserve it?" I yelled at her. She was babbling but not saying anything. I needed real answers.

"Who do you think you are, demanding an-

swers from me? I don't have to tell you shit. Just
deal with it." Her eyes tried to burn a hole
through me; unfortunately for her, I was metal
at this point.

I lost control. I ran over to her and started
beating her with my gun. I heard a bone crack
but that didn't stop me. I hit her so many more
times and with so much force that I could feel
her blood wetting my hand. Hood pulled me
off.

"Just tell her," Rich screamed at Quad. He
couldn't take me beating his sister.

But Quad was a G, or least she played the
role well. "Shut up, Rich!" she yelled back at
him with her head bobbling. She refused to give
in to me.

"Say it or I will," Rich threatened.

"Why you always got to be so weak?" she spat
at him. "Fuck it." Quad looked at me as best she
could out of her swollen eyes. "He deserved it
for what he did to my"—she swallowed. "Our father, Harold Montgomery"—she choked up. I
knew she loved her dad just as much as I loved
mine. She continued, "They were friends and
your dad turned on him over money. He shot
him and now my dad is a paraplegic, confined
to a wheelchair forever. I have watched him suffer since I was a child because of it. But I knew
that one day I would get revenge on your father.
And that day finally came.

"But in the meantime, I thought I would
have some fun and hurt others connected to
him. So I brought lover boy Rich and my
cousin Kalil along. I knew they would be able

to stir up all of your lives for a bit. And I have to admit, it was fun to watch, just as I had imagined." She tried to laugh, but it was difficult. This bitch was psycho and she had planned this all out.

"So Monica and Rochelle were a part of your sick plan? That's what these two losers were for." I pointed in the direction of Rich and Kalil.

"Of course, I knew that their troubles with your loved ones would keep you busy. All the while, I was slowly getting even. Ain't I brilliant? See, I heard about you, Mrs. Cautious. But now you will suffer just as my brother and I have."

"I guess you are brilliant, Quad. And you are right, I will suffer, but I will also thrive, bitch. Because I got the sweetest revenge a girl can get, and that is her prey."

"No, your parents were the prey. And Big Nick's clueless ass was a special bonus for sticking his nose in other people's business."

"Is that what you think?" Hood walked over and started dousing all three with gasoline.

Hood reached in his pocket and handed me a box of matches. Rich started yelling. "No, no, please, I'm sorry!" He begged like a bitch for his life.

I looked at Quad. "You see your brother begging, bitch?" Looking back at Rich, I struck a match and, without one thought, I threw it on him. Rich screamed as he flamed and burned.

"That's sweet revenge," I said to Quad as I struck another match and threw it on Kalil. Hood had beaten him so badly that his body was numb but he still screamed and moaned.

Quad watched Rich and Kalil burn and for the first time, I saw fear in her eyes. She started to squirm as if she could release herself. I just looked at her. "I'm King Kong, bitch!" I lit two matches and threw them at her. Her eyes grew larger than watermelons as she looked at the fire starting to burn her body. "Tell Lucifer about me."

She started screaming along with Rich and Kalil, whose cries were now weak as they lost consciousness. Hood handed me a mask to keep the smoke from my lungs. I watched them all until they succumbed to their burns. When they were merely ashes, Hood, C-Lo, and I exited. C-Lo set the entire house on fire.

Chapter 42

"Mmmm, I have been wanting this cup of coffee all day," Monica said as she sipped her latte. We met up at Starbucks on her lunch break.

"Girl, please, we could have been at Red Lobster but you got me up in here," I complained.

"Stop complaining, you always trying to feed your fat face." Monica smiled.

"Whatever. You know it's too hot to be drinking this mess anyway. This is not Detroit. Ain't no real winters or snow coming here. This is Florida," I reminded her.

We had been living here for seven months. Detroit was a wrap, we could no longer live there. We all agreed that Florida was a place that we could possibly call home. Things had been going good thus far. Monica graduated from school in Detroit and was now working as a paralegal at a big law firm. She wanted to become a lawyer, so she was in law school and her grades were great. I opened up a hair salon here while still owning the one in Detroit. My plan was to start a chain of salons. Rochelle was managing the one in Detroit and she loved it. They had brought in another stylist and business was booming. Rochelle was also doing real estate now. She had come into her own. The salon that I opened in Miami was booming as well. I only did a few heads, mostly athlete's wives and girlfriends. I wanted to keep that at a minimum; my focus was running the business. But doing hair was my passion, so I had to do it sometimes.

And my darling Hood was doing his thing. Finally, he was out of the dope game, completely out. I was so proud of him because he was now a real businessman. He had bought some houses and fixed them up and was a landlord. He also had two car lots, a Laundromat, and a clothing store. I knew he could do it.

"So what are you about to do?" Monica continued to sip her latte while I dreamed about food.

"Well, Hood is picking Imani up from school, then we are all going to meet at the park. Matter of fact, I better get going. I don't want to be late meeting them."

"All right. I guess I'll get a refill to go, then get on back to the office."

I was so proud of Monica. She was a respectable young woman with goals. We had come a long away from the Brewster. I wished my entire family could be here to see it, but that was not the case.

After leaving Starbucks, I swung by a local burger joint, grabbed a burger, and ate it on the way to the park where I was meeting Hood and Imani.

"Hey, babe." Hood met me at my car. I could see Imani already playing. She loved this park.

"Sorry it took so long. I was having coffee with Monica."

Imani looked up and waved at me. I waved back. She was getting so big. She had just started preschool.

"I knew you would be late anyway." Hood grinned.

"Shut up, boy," I said playfully as I sat down on a bench where I could watch Imani play.

"Come push me," Imani called out, looking in our direction.

I slowly rose back up to do it. "No, babe, sit down. I got it." Hood rose up.

"It's okay, I can do it," I protested. I enjoyed pushing Imani on the swing. Her giggle always made me laugh.

"No, babe, I want you to relax. You have to take it easy." He reached over and rubbed my protruding belly. I still could not believe that I was about to be a mom. Hood was so happy, he barely allowed me to do anything.

I knew there was no use in protesting, so I gave in. "All right, I will sit, but this bench is uncomfortable." I playfully pouted as Hood walked away. He looked back at me and smiled.

I watched Hood as he started to push Imani. She went slowly at first then fast, high in the air. Imani laughed and giggled so hard. I smiled as I watched her. I loved to see her happy. I hoped and wished it would always be this way for her and for my baby, too.

Imani giggled again, getting my attention. "Look, Auntie!" she screamed. In that moment I thought about Monica, Li'l Bo, and me as children. When we were little, Dad would take us to the park and push us high on the swings. I used to jump out when it got really high. Just thinking about it warmed my heart and I knew things would be okay for my baby and Imani. Hood looked at me and smiled.

It became clear. I had an answer to the question I had been asking myself for a long time now. Sometimes at the end of revenge's tunnel there was a light.

"My—aaaaaah!!"

hottest custom car shop, they're moving vast kilos of product faster than their scammer boss, Kirk, can pimp out rides—and living la vida luxurious. So they've got things under control when Secret and Penny's alcoholic mother shows up needing help. And when Isis' one-time love, Bobbi, begs for another chance—complete with a huge payoff—she's got his loot on lock and temptation at arm's length . . .

Chapter 1

Sometimes I wonder how my life would've turned out if my parents had been involved in different things, like if they had regular jobs. My mother would be a social worker, and my father a lawyer or something. You know, jobs they call respectable and shit.

Supposedly these people's lives are peaches and cream. But when I think about that shit I laugh, because my life is way different. My father was a dope pusher who served the whole area of Detroit. And when I say the whole area, I mean just that. My dad served some of the wealthiest politicians all the way down to the poorest people in the hood who would do anything for a fix. Needless to say, if you were on cocaine before my father went to prison, I'm sure he served you; he was heavy in the street. Lester

Bedford was his birth name, and that's what he went by in the streets of Detroit. And there was no one who would fuck with him. Everybody was in check.

All the dudes on the block were jealous of him because his pockets were laced. He had the looks, money, nice cars, and the baddest chick on the block, Marisa Haywood. All the dudes wanted Marisa because she was a redbone with coal-black hair flowing down her back and a banging-ass body, but she was only interested in my dad. They had met one night at a friend's dice party and had been inseparable since then.

Life was good for them for a long time. Dad was able to make a lot of money with no hassle from the feds, and Mom was able to stay home with their three kids. Three beautiful kids, if I may say so. First, she had me, Mya, then my brother, Bobby, who we all call Li'l Bo, and last was my baby sister, Monica.

We were all happy kids about four years ago; we didn't need or want for nothing. My daddy made sure of that. The only thing my father wanted to give us next was a house with a back-yard. Even though he was stacking good dough, we still lived in the Brewster-Douglass Projects.

All those years he'd been trying to live by the hood code. However, times were changing. The new and upcoming ballers were getting their dough and moving out of the hood. Around this time my dad decided to take us outta there too.

Before he could make a move, our good luck suddenly changed for the worse. Our apartment was raided by the feds. After sitting in jail for six months, his case finally went to court, where he received a life sentence with no possibility of parole.

My mother never told us what happened, but sometimes I would eavesdrop on her conversations when she would be crying on a friend's shoulder. That's how I overheard her saying that they had my father connected to six drug-related murders and indicted on cocaine charges. I couldn't believe my ears. My father wouldn't kill anybody. He was too nice for that. I was completely pissed off; I refused to hear any of that. It was a lie. As far as I was concerned, my father was no murderer and all that shit he was accused of was somebody's sick fantasy. He was innocent. They were just jealous of him because he was young, black, and borderline rich. True, it was drug money, but in the hood, who gave a fuck. But all that was in the past; now, my dad was on skid row. Lockdown. Three hots and a cot. And our home life reflected just that.

All of a sudden my mother started hanging out all night. She would come home just in time for us to go to school. For a while that was okay, but then her behavior also started to change. I mean, my mother looked totally different. Her once-healthy skin started to look pale and dry. She started to lose weight, and her hair was never combed. She tried to comb it, but this was a woman who was used to going to the beauty shop every week. Now her hair looked like that of a stray cat.

I noticed things missing out of the house, too, like our Alpine digital stereo. I came home from school one day and it was gone. I asked my mother about it, and she said she sold it for food. But that had to be a lie because we were on the county. Mom didn't work, so we received food stamps and cash assistance. We also received government assistance that paid the rent, but Mom was responsible for the utilities, which started to get shut off.

Before long, we looked like the streets. After my father had been locked up for two years, we had nothing. We started to outgrow our clothes because Mom couldn't afford to buy us any, so whatever secondhand clothes we could get, we wore. I'm talking about some real stinking-looking gear. Li'l Bo got suspended from school for kicking some boy's ass about teasing him about a shirt he wore to school with someone else's name on it. We had been too wrapped up in our new home life to realize it. When the lady from the Salvation Army came over with the clothes for Li'l Bo, he just ironed the shirt and put it on. He never realized the spray paint on the back of the shirt said *Alvin*. That is, until this asshole at school decided to point it out to him.

Everything of value in our house was gone. Word on the streets was my mother was a crackhead and prostitute. I tried to deny it at first, but before long, it became obvious.

Now it's been four years of this mess, and I just can't take it anymore. I don't know what to do. I'm only seventeen years old. I'm sitting here on this couch hungry with nothing to eat and my mom is lying up in her room with some nigga for a lousy few bucks. And when she's done, she's going to leave here and cop some more dope. I'm just sick of this.

"Li'l Bo, Monica," I shouted so they could hear me clearly. "Come on, let's go to the store so we can get something to eat."

"I don't want to go to the store, Mya. It's cold out there," Monica said, pouting as she came out of the room we shared.

"Look, put your shoes on. I'm not leaving you here without me or Li'l Bo. Besides, ain't nothing in that kitchen to eat so if we don't go to the store, we starve tonight."

"Well, let's go. I ain't got all night." Li'l Bo tried to rush us, shifting side to side where he stood. The only thing he cares about is that video game that he has to hide to keep Mom from selling.

On our way to the store we passed all the local wannabe dope boys on our block. As usual, they couldn't resist hitting on me. But I never pay them losers any mind because I will never mess around with any of them. Most of the grimy niggas been sleeping with my mom anyway. Especially Squeeze, with his bald-headed ass. Nasty bastard. If I had a gun I would probably shoot all them niggas.

"Hey, Mya. Girl, you know you growing up. Why don't you let me take you up to Roosters and buy you a burger or something?" Squeeze asked while rubbing his bald head and licking his nasty, hungry lips at me. "With a fat ass like that, girl, I will let you order whatever you want off the menu."

"Nigga, I don't need you to buy me jack. I'm good." I rolled my eyes and kept stepping.

"Whatever, bitch, wit' yo' high and mighty ass. You know you hungry."

Li'l Bo stopped dead in his tracks. "What you call my sister?" He turned around and mugged Squeeze. "Can you hear, nigga? I said, what did you call my sister?" Li'l Bo spat the words at Squeeze.

I grabbed Li'l Bo by the arm. "Come on, don't listen to him. He's just talkin'. Forget him anyway." I dismissed Squeeze with a wave of my hand.

"Yeah, little man, I'm only playing." Squeeze had an ugly scowl on his face.

Before I walked away I turned around and threw up my middle finger to Squeeze because that nigga's time is coming. He's got plenty of enemies out here on the streets while he's wasting time fooling with me.

When we made it to the store I told Li'l Bo and Monica to watch my back while I got some food. I picked up some sandwich meat, cheese, bacon, and hot dogs. I went to the counter and paid for a loaf of bread to make it look legit, and then we left the store. Once outside, we hit the store right next door. I grabbed some canned goods, a pack of Oreo cookies for dessert, and two packs of chicken wings. When we got outside, we unloaded all the food into the shopping bags we brought from home. That would get us through until next week. This is how we eat because Mom sells all the food stamps every damn month. The thought of it made me kick a single rock that was in my path while walking back to the Brewster.

When we got back to the house, Mom was in the kitchen rambling like she's looking for something. So she must be finished doing her dirty business. I walked right past her like she ain't even standing there.

"Where the hell y'all been? Don't be leavin' this house at night without telling me," she screamed, then flicked some cigarette butts into the kitchen sink.

"We went to the store to get food. There is nothin' to eat in this damn house." I rolled my eyes, giving her much attitude.

"Mya, who the hell do you think you talking to? I don't care where you went. Tell me before you leave this house," she said, while sucking her teeth.

"Yeah, whatever! If you cared so much, we would have food." I got smart again. "Monica, grab the skillet so I can fry some of this chicken," I ordered her, then slammed the freezer door shut.

Mom paused for a minute. She was staring at me so hard I thought she was about to slap me for real. But she just turned around and went to her room. Then she came right back out of her room and went into the bathroom with clothes in hand.

I knew she was going to leave when she got that money from her little trick. Normally, I want her to stay in the house. That way I know she's safe. But tonight, I'm ready for her to leave because I'm pissed at her right now. I still love her, but I don't understand what happened to her so fast. Things have been hard on all of us. Why does she get to take the easy way out by doing crack? I just wish Dad was here, but he's not, so I got to do something to take care of my brother and sister and get us out of this rathole.

Chapter 1

*P*op. *Pop. Pop.*

"Agh!" I screamed as the hot bullet that left Luscious's gun pierced my left shoulder. Grabbing my shoulder, I instantly felt the hot blood start dripping down my sleeve. But the thud of Luscious's body hitting the ground had my attention. Then Luscious disappeared and on the ground in his spot Monica lay covered in blood. "MONICA, MONICA!!" I yelled over and over.

"Mya!" I heard someone yelling my name, but my body was frozen in one spot. Panic set in as I tried to force myself toward Monica. "Mya," I heard my name again. I felt myself blacking out.

"Mya." I finally opened my eyes and realized it was Hood shaking me, calling my name. "Babe, it's only a dream again. You at home and safe. So is Monica." I looked around the room as I realized I was home in my bed. "Shit, I hate these dreams." I sat up then slightly, pushed my Donna Karan stitched quilt off me, and climbed out of the bed. Realizing I had interrupted Hood's sleep again, I apologized. "And I'm really sorry for waking you up with this shit again." I went into our master bathroom to wipe all the perspiration off my forehead that had built up while I was panicking in my dreaming.

"It's a'ight, you know I got you. Besides I'm 'bout to get up anyway. Gotta handle business." As usual, I could always count on Hood to be supportive. No matter what. But I was sick of having these dreams. It had been well over a year since Luscious had tried to sneak up on me at Stylz by Design to take me out. He thought he had me too, but his plan had failed when Monica came out of nowhere and shot him in the back of the head, killing him instantly. I was lucky, because had it not been for my sister Monica, I would be dead. Luscious did end up shooting me in the shoulder, but I recovered so fast it was like a pat on the back. To be honest, the dreams were worse than getting shot.

The only regret I had about the whole incident was Monica getting caught up in the middle. I hated that she now had murder on her hands. Even worse, it was her daughter Imani's father that she had killed. It was only a coincidence that she had even showed up at the shop that morning. On her way to school she remembered she needed money. She later said that she had attempted to call my cell but got no answer so she came because she knew that was where I would be. As she pulled in, she happened to see Luscious, who she thought was dead, slip into my shop. Monica said she knew he was up to something and without a second thought she grabbed the .22 pistol that Hood had given her for protection out of the glove compartment of her all-white 2012 Dodge Charger. Just as she entered the back of the shop, she saw me running toward Luscious as he fired shots at me. So even though I regret her having to kill Imani's dad, I thank God that she did.

As I came out of the bathroom, Hood headed into our triple-sized walk-in closet. "Well, since I'm up, would you like me to make you some breakfast? A little eggs, bacon, maybe some hash browns," I offered. There was no way I was going back to sleep. I refused to close my eyes only to get a glimpse of Luscious. Hell no. I would stay woke.

I had told Rochelle I was coming in late today since I stayed over the night before, but what the heck, I might as well drag my ass in. I could get an early start on inventory since I didn't have any appointments scheduled. Even though I owned the shop, I still had a few special clients. And for my services they paid top dollar.

"Nah, babe, I'm good. I'ma meet up with my people early this morning so I'll just grab some on the way." Hood walked into the bathroom as I plopped back down on the bed and quietly contemplated my next move. I decided a latte would do me good so I made the kitchen a part of my mission for the morning. Not soon after

Hood left the house I jumped in the shower. An hour later I had searched through my closet and fished out a pair of white Vince tennis shorts with a black Helmut Lang tank. I completed the outfit with Alexander Wang ankle-strap sandals. I had to admit my new style was classic. I had put the Brewster Projects dressing behind me. At least a little bit—I still would represent from time to time. With not as much as one glance in the mirror, I concluded I was ready to head out.

HIGH PRAISE FOR ALAN RUSSELL AND *MULTIPLE WOUNDS*!

"Russell allows his exquisitely flawed characters to follow a vertiginous plot to its logical conclusion. Readers who enjoy intelligent repartee at the scene of the crime will find *Multiple Wounds* enlightening as well as entertaining."

—*St. Petersburg Times*

"Entertaining... Action moving... A conclusion that brings all the pieces of the puzzle together. Russell makes the most of the imaginative setup."

—*Chicago Tribune*

"[An] ambitious attempt to push the boundaries of the crime novel."

—*The Los Angeles Times*

"A searing multilayered thriller that hits all the marks."

—Michael Connelly

"A tour de force."

—*Kirkus Reviews*

"Russell offers up a highly original, literate mystery that is part psychological thriller, part exploration of the human soul, and part police procedural...a top-notch choice."

—*Booklist*

"An extremely rewarding voyage. Russell has produced his most ambitious and imaginative novel to date, a skillful mix of thrills both intellectual and visceral."

—*The San Diego Union-Tribune*

"Alan Russell's *Multiple Wounds* is a triumph of inventiveness and suspense. On no accounts should it be missed."

—*The Armchair Detective*

MORE PRAISE FOR ALAN RUSSELL AND *MULTIPLE WOUNDS*!

"This multilayered plot is as tightly coiled as a spring-loaded booby-trap. The plot builds and stretches as taut as an acrobat's high-wire. Russell's characterizations are superb. I highly recommend *Multiple Wounds*. It is an extraordinary suspense thriller by an author who has the gift of revealing the masks people wear to hide from each other and from themselves."

—*Tulsa World*

"This is Russell's most mature novel, tackling the issue of suffering in its many guises."

—*Publishers Weekly*

"Alan Russell continues his love affair with language in a mature new dimension in *Multiple Wounds*...a book which requires thoughtful reading, and has advanced our praise for and expectations of Alan Russell and his writing."

—Mystgalaxy.com

MORE PRAISE FOR ALAN RUSSELL
AND *MULTIPLE WOUNDS*!

"This multilayered plot is as tightly coiled as a spring-loaded booby-trap. The plot builds and stretches as taut as an acrobat's high-wire. Russell's characterizations are superb. I highly recommend *Multiple Wounds*. It is an extraordinary suspense thriller by an author who has the gift of revealing the masks people wear to hide from each other and from themselves."

—*Tulsa World*

"This is Russell's most mature novel, tackling the issue of suffering in its many guises."

—*Publishers Weekly*

"Alan Russell continues his love affair with language in a mature new dimension in *Multiple Wounds*...a book which requires thoughtful reading, and has advanced our praise for and expectations of Alan Russell and his writing."

—Mystgalaxy.com